THAT SATURDAY
FEELING

THAT SATURDAY FEELING

•

INGRID BETZ

AVALON BOOKS
THOMAS BOUREGY AND COMPANY, INC.
401 LAFAYETTE STREET
NEW YORK, NEW YORK 10003

PRINTED IN THE UNITED STATES OF AMERICA
ON ACID-FREE PAPER
BY HADDON CRAFTSMEN, BLOOMSBURG, PENNSYLVANIA

THAT SATURDAY
FEELING

Chapter One

"I know Rene's friend the wildlife man will be here to house-sit. But would you keep an eye on things while we're gone? The carpets, the Royal Copenhagen, and don't forget Saint Francis over there . . ." Margaret waved fond fingers at the seventeenth-century wood carving communing with its reflection in the dresser mirror.

"Of course I will. Stop worrying."

"I mean aside from having your staff continue the weekly cleaning. If you could drop by yourself now and again. Just to check and see the house and its contents aren't being, well—abused?"

"You *are* worried, aren't you?"

March Briarwood gave her older sister an affectionate look. People were always saying how similar they were. Slim-figured, with glossy black hair and eyes seductively almond-shaped. Only Margaret's hair was cut fashionably short while her own swung in two crescent arcs to frame her oval face, and Margaret's eyes were a cool sapphire while hers were a hyacinth shade of blue. Of course Margaret went in for makeup, lots of it exquisitely applied, and designer-label clothes to complement her position as part-owner of the exclusive downtown art gallery she ran with her husband.

They were in the apricot-and-cream master bedroom

where Margaret was packing for a three-month buying trip she and Rene were taking to Europe. Open suitcases stood on the alpaca wool rug. The satin bedspread on the king-sized bed was buried under Alfred Sung suits, and frothy peach lingerie that March would have been embarrassed to wear under her sensible gray flannel skirt and navy jacket. She'd been doing inspections across town for Marchmaids Inc., her firm of professional home cleaners, when Margaret's voice came over the car phone.

She needed to talk—just the two of them. Any chance March could spare half an hour and drop by The Cedars? "As if you had to ask!" said March, and canceled the rest of her afternoon. As far back as she could remember, they'd been there for each other. Sharing homework, clothes, confidences. Sympathy when romances turned sour—money when jobs ran out. They were sisters who'd gone far together.

"Are you saying you don't trust this what's-his-name—this friend of Rene's?"

"Hunter J. Reynolds." Margaret glanced distractedly at a sleeveless chiffon confection and returned it reluctantly to the closet. "Too summery for September. Oh, I'm sure he pays his taxes and brushes his teeth and all the rest of it. He's a wildlife biologist, actually—tops in his field, Rene says. But my choice as house sitter for The Cedars? No way!"

"Fascinating! Tell me more."

March stuffed another satin pillow behind her and leaned back on the bed. Margaret and Rene Vermeer were the most perfectly matched couple she knew. In spite of an age difference between them of nearly twenty years, they normally saw eye to eye on everything. From the pricey canvases for sale in their gallery, to a sinfully haute cuisine taste in restaurants, to their eclectic circle of friends.

"It's his lifestyle I don't trust. Footloose and rootless are adjectives that spring to mind. The man's spent more years in tents and igloos than he has under a solid roof. Boiling tea over campfires and decoding the mating habits of hoary marmots, or what tundra wolves eat in January—that type of stuff."

March laughed. She could just imagine. A leathery faced old loner accustomed to tossing the tea leaves out the canvas door. Not her urban sister's scene, and definitely no match for a house full of cream carpeting and sophisticated art.

"You've met him, I gather?"

Margaret turned to the bed with a pastel armful of silk blouses. "Once. On a buying trip to British Columbia. The time we brought back that fabulous Emily Carr?" She began folding with the ease of long practice. "Hunter insisted on giving us a personal tour of Saltspring Island. I had nightmares about trees for weeks after! Oh, don't get me wrong—he's got charm if you like the laid-back kind. And he's probably great to have around if there's a grizzly after you. When Rene heard he was coming to Weatherfield U as a guest lecturer, he leaped at the chance to have him stay at the house."

"Maybe he's tired of wood smoke and marmots and he's converting to civilization. You've got to admit, Maggie, it's not a bad idea. Having somebody stay here while you're gone. Alarm systems aren't foolproof."

"No. But neither are houseguests." She held up a sassy black cocktail number with a swooping décolletage. "What do you think? Yes or no?"

"Yes, by all means." March sighed and allowed herself a moment's raging envy. "To think you're actually going places where you get to wear things like that!"

The sapphire eyes flashed her a look. "It's your own fault that you're not. Living like a nun! You've done nothing but work since you slammed the door on Kent Harrison. A social life doesn't fall from the sky, you know. You've got to make it happen. Get out, go places!"

"Maggie, be fair! I went to the movies just last week." Which was no answer, but the best she could come up with on short notice.

"Alone, I suppose. And don't call me Maggie! I hate that old name. You'll never get to wear items like this to the movies," she said with feeling, as the dress disappeared into her case under a layer of tissue paper. "Seriously, March. Rene and I worry about you. You're all of twenty-seven and it's been nearly a year now since Kent. When are you going to give some other lucky man a chance to take you out?"

"You know the answer. When I find a man who interests me as much as running a business does." They'd had this argument before, with lively variations, but why spoil the afternoon? She glanced at her watch and muttered, not quite truthfully, "Is that the time? I promised Anna Rose I'd be back at the office by five."

"I've said too much, haven't I? Your love life, or lack of it, is none of my business . . ."

"True. But I'd miss it if you didn't." March grinned as they walked under the skylight in the atrium. It wasn't often she got to see a contrite look on her sister's face. "I'd think you didn't care. Catch you and Rene at the airport Saturday?"

"Yes. That reminds me—I want to give you some postdated checks for the cleaning. It's been crazy lately, what with packing, and breaking in the temporary manager we hired. You won't forget?" she whispered, giving March a hug. Her glance brushed the fountain splashing on the marble tiles, and the graceful shape of Venetian glass visible through the living-room arch. "About the house? I'd rather not mention it in front of Rene . . ."

"I won't. I promise. I know how you feel about The Cedars."

And why shouldn't she? It was the same way March felt about the little gabled cottage they'd grown up in—the one she'd fought so hard to keep, and woe to anyone who posed a threat to it. They were alike in more than just looks. At the big oak door, she paused.

"When's he arriving, anyway? The man who lives with wolves?"

Margaret winced. "A day or two after we leave. He's driving from Vancouver so he couldn't say exactly."

March nodded. "I'll give him till Monday noon and then I'll call. Make sure he got here and is settling in."

But she didn't have to. Hunter J. Reynolds called her first.

She was sitting at her desk in the Marchmaids office, making Monday morning adjustments to the schedule with Anna Rose, her staff supervisor, when the telephone rang. It was nine on the dot.

"Hunt Reynolds here. At the Vermeers? What's keeping you people?" enquired a casual voice. "I've been in the house since last night and there's no sign of a maid.''

March frowned. Was she supposed to call him Mr. Reynolds, Professor, or what? And what did he mean, *maid?*

''Welcome to Weatherfield,'' she said, stalling while she swiveled round to double-check. ''The Cedars is down for Saturday. Nine A.M. to twelve noon.'' He had some awful brass music blaring in the background and she was forced to speak up. ''Margaret preferred that day. But if you'd like to pick another . . .''

He sounded bemused. ''Maybe we should take this conversation from the top. Call me Hunt. And you're . . . ?''

''March Briarwood.'' She let a touch of disparagement filter through her voice. First names were not a good idea with customers—especially male customers, as she'd discovered to her cost with Kent. ''I own the agency.''

''March Maids. Clever! Let me get this straight. You're saying the maid only comes over once a week?''

Light dawned as she shifted her gaze to the corner window, where a steady rain was pelting the cars on Emery Street. ''Marchmaids isn't a maid service, if that's what you're thinking. We're a cleaning agency. Didn't Margaret leave you a note?''

''Cleaning ladies! Glad we cleared that up!'' He laughed, not at all bothered. ''Yes, there's a note. But I seem to have spilled coffee on it.''

March exchanged glances with Anna Rose, who was smothering amusement on the other side of the desk. ''Cleaners, we're called nowadays, Professor

Reynolds. Of course, if you think you'll require our services more often, we'd be—''

''Heck no! It's just that I tracked a bit of mud onto the carpet, moving in. Nothing that won't keep till Saturday. Nice meeting you, March,'' he told her amicably, and hung up. She replaced the receiver feeling like a cat whose fur had been rubbed the wrong way.

''If you could stop giggling for a minute, what do you think? Should we take a chance? By Saturday the dirt could be ground in.''

''Andrea's in the change room. Her first customer canceled. Why don't we send her over with the rug steamer, no charge?''

March nodded, relieved at the simplicity of the solution, and Anna Rose's plump figure slipped across the hall into the room where the staff had their lockers. She heard Andrea's boyish shouts of laughter punctuate the clatter of equipment as the two women wrestled the steamer out of its lair under the stairs. Evidently she found the idea of being mistaken for a maid hilarious.

March wasn't so sure. She hoped the mistake wasn't a sign of unrealistic expectations on Hunter Reynolds's part. A man could build up all kinds of strange ideas during long years alone in the wild.

''You've got that dust-on-the-baseboards look on your face,'' said Anna Rose, back in her chair. ''You're not still fussing, are you?''

March sighed.

''He sounded friendly enough.'' She couldn't seem to get his voice out of her ear. Warm and relaxed, and vibrating with deep male timbre. ''Only he wasn't taking things very seriously. Margaret warned me he might not. Maybe I should have taken the steamer over there myself.''

"For a few muddy footprints? Give the man a chance to do something wrong first.''

"You're right. I'm overreacting.'' Embarrassing if he thought she was spying on him! She leaned over the schedule. "Where were we? Oh, yes. Freda Walmsley called, could we fit her in Thursday, her bridge club's coming. Somebody with a twelve-room bed and breakfast wants their Venetians washed yesterday. And Cindy needs more time to find a sitter for the new baby before she comes back to work.''

Anna Rose groaned and reached for a pen. "It's going to be one of those weeks. One crisis after another.''

March grinned. "You mean challenge, don't you?'' The kind they could really sink their teeth into. Forget Hunter Reynolds. He was probably exaggerating anyway about the mud, with the wrongheaded notion that he could wangle full-time maid service out of them.

She put him firmly out of her mind. Where he stayed until Saturday when she arrived home from the supermarket to find Anna Rose's white hatchback still parked in the driveway. Saturdays were half-holidays for Marchmaids and normally by one o'clock all the women had gone home.

Anna Rose, still in her blue-and-white wraparound apron, was dancing on the step, signaling disaster.

"March, you've got to do something about that man! We're losing all our staff!''

"What man? What do you mean, losing?'' She dropped her grocery bags in the hall outside the office, trying to make sense of Anna Rose's agitated explanations.

"Hunter Reynolds! With the muddy feet? I just got back from driving Cheryl to the emergency clinic. She's all right, but—"

"Emergency?" The pine-paneled walls swayed and March felt for the edge of the desk. "Tell me everything. From the beginning."

"Liz and Cheryl were doing The Cedars this morning. Like always. Halfway through I get a call from Liz. Frantic! Seems Cheryl went in to start the kitchen and found this pack of chipmunks—"

"Chipmunks!" echoed March. Could she really be hearing this? "You mean those small striped rodents? With the stand-up tails? In the *kitchen?*"

"In the cupboard. The one with the staples? They'd gotten into the flour and the sugar and were starting on the cereal—"

"But how did they get into the kitchen? From outside?"

"From a cage. Where Professor Reynolds had them locked up. Only they must have gotten loose. One of them bit Cheryl on the leg when she got between him and a cornflakes box."

March sank into the swivel chair, her blue paisley skirt billowing out over the armrest. She felt a wild desire to laugh, except that the situation was anything but funny. "Cheryl's not badly hurt, you said?"

"Suffering from shock mainly, the doctor said. I ran her over to the clinic for a rabies shot, just in case."

March nodded. Trust Anna Rose to do the right thing. "And Liz? Is she all right?"

"Fine. Except that she's quitting. March, they both are! Cheryl says this proves she should have gone into hairdressing and Liz decided she's retiring." Anna

Rose's voice rose on a note of desperation. "Now what do we do?"

March ran fingers through her hair distractedly. Liz was her senior cleaner, a five-feet-two dynamo she would have trusted with the Taj Mahal. "She can't mean that! It's just the reaction . . ."

"I don't think so. She was talking about joining her sister in Florida. 'I'm too old to see what that man is doing to that beautiful house'—those were her words."

"Doing?" interrupted March. He'd been there for less than a week, for heaven's sake! "What else is he doing besides haboring wildlife? You were there! What did the house look like?"

"I was only in the kitchen. We didn't want to risk the chipmunks getting out so we kept the door shut." Anna Rose looked evasive. "Liz mentioned pizza boxes and spilled pop cans. She said he had to be bringing students home from the university."

"Students *and* wildlife? That does it! I don't care if he *is* Rene's friend!" March flipped open the telephone book. "There must be a law! So help me, I'll get City Hall after him—Animal Control—" Her finger was partway down the column of municipal numbers when Anna Rose laid a hand on hers. "March? Before you call? Professor Reynolds left a message on the answering machine."

"Apologizing, you mean?"

March reached over, activated the tape, and waited impatiently while it ran squealing backwards. "He'll have to do better than that before I'm through with him." She stabbed the forward button and Anna Rose mumbled that he wasn't apologizing exactly, just as the deep voice she was beginning to dislike intensely announced, "Hunter Reynolds. I want to register a complaint."

March gasped.

"A couple, in fact. I walk in the door and find my animals loose and the kitchen looking like a tornado touched down. What in heck were you people playing at here? I'm close—this close—to reporting you to the Better Business Bureau."

"That's outrageous! I don't have to listen to this," declared March, but Anna Rose insisted, "I think you'd better. It gets worse."

"Or the Humane Society," he was saying. "Believe me, if one of those chipmunks had been injured, I would!"

"What about injury to my staff?" March yelled at the machine.

"It's obvious. One of your staff got careless and opened the cage door—"

"As if!" hissed Anna Rose. "Liz and Cheryl are scared of anything on legs that doesn't talk."

"—and then panicked and took off. Leaving this unholy mess. I don't give a thin dime whose sister you are." The resonant male voice expressed scorn for irrelevant details. "Unless you get somebody over here to clean up and pretty darn fast, *Ms.* Briarwood, don't bother trying to collect this week's check."

"The checks!" March's shoulders slumped. She felt as though the wind had been knocked out of her. "They're at The Cedars. Margaret forgot to give them to me. You realize he's got us over a barrel?" She groaned. The Vermeers were her largest account. "But it's not just the money! I promised my sister she'd have the same house to come back to that she left."

She'd go through fire and water rather than let Margaret and Rene down. Her sister had kept a roof over their heads and food on the table in those early years after a plane crash had claimed their parents' lives. Later when March needed capital to finance her growing business, Rene had been the one who guaranteed her loan at the bank. She stood up and took a restless turn around the room.

"What's this Hunter Reynolds like in person? Did the women say?"

"They never laid eyes on him. Apparently he has a morning class on Saturdays. Listen, why don't I go over there right now?" Anna Rose dug in a capacious pocket for her car keys and started for the change room. "Half an hour and I'll have the kitchen spic and span."

"You of all people! With a brand-new husband and a house of your own to take care of. You've already given the professor half your afternoon off, in case you hadn't noticed."

"I don't mind. Tony's working at the garage till five. As staff supervisor, I feel responsible . . ."

"Let him stew. Do him good," said March, resentment rising as her brain replayed his unfair accusations. "If anybody goes, it'll be me. And not just to clean! It's time I set Nature Boy straight and laid down a few ground rules."

Anna Rose sent her a sidelong look—she was familiar with that tone of voice. "If you're sure." She dropped her apron in the laundry bin and took a checked jacket out of her locker. "Maybe it's not such a bad idea, you going over. He's a man, isn't he?" She grinned. "Who knows! Once he sets eyes on you in person, he may say to heck with the kitchen, and take you dining and dancing instead."

"Dreamer!"

March shook her head fondly as Anna Rose moved to the mirror to pat the thick chestnut coil of hair that was her best feature.

"Hunter Reynolds isn't a man. He's a wildlife biologist. His idea of dining and dancing is most likely freeze-dried eggs and ring-around-the-campfire."

She had been piecing his picture together ever since Margaret first mentioned him and it didn't add up to anyone she was keen to know socially. "He's probably programmed to register four-legged vertebrates only. I'll be lucky if he doesn't come after me with a canoe paddle! And since he's Rene's friend and Rene's over fifty, he could well be pushing retirement. Why else is he trading the wilds for the university? Besides which—" She sighed, aware of a nagging sense of discontent. "—Saturday is my night to do the books. You know that."

Anna Rose paused at the door. Her face, transparent as freshly washed glass, was full of disapproval. "It's not right, what you're doing to yourself. Making business the be-all and end-all of your existence."

"You're too late! I had that lecture from Margaret before she left." March waited on the step while Anna Rose climbed into her car, the twin of her own. "See you Monday?"

"Eight sharp. Have the coffee on." Anna Rose turned the key in the ignition and let the motor idle. "Are you sure you're not still pining for that awful Kent Harrison?"

"Pining, no. Still angry, yes. And wiser. Are you leaving yet, so I can tackle the professor?"

"Sorry. It's just that—" She waved a helpless hand and March felt herself soften. "I know. Now that you're living on cloud nine with your Tony, you think it should be the same for everybody.''

She watched the hatchback make the turn into Emery Street.

Anna Rose had been the first cleaner she'd hired. The floors they'd polished and the sinks they'd scoured in an effort to get the fledgling business off the ground! In the process, they'd become best friends. In June, Anna Rose had married her high school sweetheart, curly-haired Tony Tremonti, and March had to admit they made a radiant advertisement for love and marriage. Three years ago, when Kent Harrison entered her life, she had entertained notions in that direction herself. Until the night of the Weatherfield Life banquet, when their final humiliating exchange had put an end to that delusion.

March sighed and let the warmth of the September sun submerge the lingering chill of the memory. The maple next door was turning color, and the dahlias edging her front lawn were at their mauve-and-crimson best. She loved this older neighborhood of the city, with its modest blue-collar homes set under tall shade trees. She and Margaret had grown up here on Emery Street, in the gabled gray cottage with the gingerbread fascia trim and white-painted shutters. When Marchmaids needed an office and change and supply rooms, she'd converted the downstairs rather than move somewhere new.

Her glance sought the circular blue-and-white plaque beside the door as she let herself in. On it a marching maid, skirt swinging, shouldered a mop musket-fashion. Marchmaids against the world! She'd felt a lot of that in the early years. Some days not much had changed, she thought, and headed for the telephone.

He wasn't able to come to the phone right now. With great charm and sincerity, Hunter Reynolds suggested she leave her name and number at the sound of the beep and he'd get back to her.

March expelled an impatient breath. Two could play the answering machine messages game!

"March Briarwood returning your call," she informed him briskly. "We don't normally work Saturday afternoons. But I can have a team over there first thing Monday. About the chipmunks—" She struggled to keep her tone businesslike. "Your animals were already in the kitchen when my staff arrived. One of the women required medical attention after being bitten on the leg. As a result, Marchmaids is now minus the services of two excellent cleaners and I'm holding you responsible. I think we should talk, don't you?" She hung up.

"Ball in your court, Professor," she muttered, scooping up her groceries on the way to the kitchen.

Sheer luck, the eggs hadn't broken when she'd dropped the bags. Clearing away the mugs accumulated around the coffeemaker, she unpacked her purchases. Macaroni and cheese again tonight, she supposed. The thing she missed most about Kent Harrison was being invited to a restaurant for a meal she didn't have to cook herself. Did Hunter Reynolds cook? she wondered, grating cheddar. Or did he eat out a lot like Kent? Margaret hadn't mentioned a woman in his life. Footloose and rootless, she'd called him. If there *had* been a woman, he'd left her behind years ago. She frowned at the pasta bubbling in the saucepan. Right from the start the man had irritated her, even when she knew next to nothing about him.

She slid the casserole into the oven and started on a salad.

Across the yard, a single bloom on her father's old rosebush glowed creamy white in the late-afternoon sun. Blanche Mallerin, her father said it was—an enchanted name belonging to a princess in a fairy tale, she'd thought as a child, imagining herself as the princess. The kitchen, too, was full of the gentle presence of the past. Over the years, favorite pieces of family furniture had found their way into the room. Her mother's maple dinette set, her father's tweed rocker dozing in the window alcove, the cranberry glass her grandmother collected, arranged on narrow shelves across the panes for the sun to catch and interspersed with tiny pots of ivy and flowering kalanchoe.

Flowers for Cheryl might be a nice gesture. Tomorrow she'd order some. She'd have to compose an ad as well, to post in the Employment Center. All because of Hunter Reynolds! With Cindy not back yet, her staff was down to a minimum six and no spares. She pondered the wording as she laid her solitary placemat and knife and fork on the table.

Agency requires cleaner. Energetic, dependable . . . That was how she usually started. She jotted down the phrases as the aroma of baking cheese wafted through the kitchen.

Mulling over what she'd written later in the office, she added *Must be comfortable around animals. And teenagers* wouldn't hurt either. The Clendennings had four, all into sports, and Anna Rose rotated the teams assigned to them in an effort to prevent burnout. The phone rang and absently she picked it up.

"Marchmaids. May I help you?"

"Live this time, are we?"

Adrenaline pumped through her veins. "If you're thinking of making that another complaint, Professor Reynolds—"

"Not at all. I'm calling to apologize."

"Oh. Really?" Cautiously she lowered her pen. He had violins playing in the background. A soothing, sunny sound.

"I'm sorry to hear one of your staff was bitten. Chipmunks are normally very shy. Not into aggression at all. It makes me wonder what the young woman was doing to provoke an attack."

"Provoke!" She might have known he'd twist things around. "That's about as absurd as suggesting my cleaners opened the cage. You won't find better trained or more conscientious personnel anywhere."

"Even assuming I agreed with you—which obviously at the moment I don't—what good would it do me? Since they're not available when I need them. Monday is too late, Ms. Briarwood. I want this mess cleaned up by tomorrow."

She tightened her grip on the receiver. "We're not a twenty-four-hour housekeeping service, Professor Reynolds. I believe it's time we discussed exactly what it is we do provide."

"Suits me. Drop by, why don't you? We can talk while you clean. And since we're talking fine print— doesn't it state somewhere in your policy charter, 'satisfaction guaranteed'?"

She flushed. Very sharp, for a man who'd spent his life in the woods. "That doesn't apply with wild animals on the premises. You realize if Rene and Margaret had the slightest inkling—"

"It's up to us to make sure they don't, isn't it? For

your sake as well as mine.'' His tone was dry. Worse
still, it hinted at amusement. ''I doubt your sister
would be happy to see how Marchmaids Inc. is looking after her beautiful home.''

She drew a difficult breath. ''That's a low blow,
Professor Reynolds. Right next door to blackmail, in
fact.''

''Is it? I don't know . . .'' He heaved a sigh that
made him sound almost human. ''It seems like a fair
trade to me. You fulfill your cleaning obligations.
Take home your check. And neither of us says anything about what happened here today.'' He paused
while she thought hostile thoughts. ''I'm a desperate
man, Ms. Briarwood,'' he said softly. ''The fact is,
I've invited a few people over for dinner tomorrow
night.''

She remembered the pizza boxes and pop cans.
''What kind of people?'' she asked sharply.

''In a moment of reckless goodwill, the dean of the
university and his wife. Friends of the Vermeers, I
understand.''

So they were. *He* was a dear but she was an awful
gossip, Margaret had once confided. Beaten on all
counts, thought March. It was the way Hunt Reynolds
had gone about it that she objected to. She unclenched
her fingers from around the telephone cord.

''Is ten o'clock tomorrow morning too early?''

''Heck no! Make it seven if you prefer.'' His grin
came down the wire, as impudent as though he were
standing opposite her. ''Have the women use their key
if I'm still in bed. Tell them to put the coffee on while
they're at it.''

She added another unflattering stroke to an image
already overloaded with them. ''Ten,'' she said coldly.
''I'll be over myself.''

Chapter Two

Parkway Drive was one of Weatherfield's most sought-after addresses, winding between princely homes set well back on acres of green. In summer the roses were spectacular.

Now russet and gold asters bloomed in pots on colonnaded porticoes, and branch by branch, the beeches were catching fire. Through the treetops, March glimpsed the mellow battlements of the university tower. A squirrel scampered out in the Sunday quiet from under the tall hedge that gave The Cedars its name. Another of the professor's little friends? she wondered, signal light flashing as she turned into the driveway.

The house was all soaring roof lines and angular expanses of tinted glass held together by honey-brown cedar shakes. The architect's fees alone, Margaret had hinted, would have been enough to build the cottage on Emery Street. Strategic plantings of juniper and sandcherry gave it the illusion of growing naturally out of its surroundings. Parked on the interlocking brick in front of the garage was a classy red Range Rover with a British Columbia license plate.

March felt a tremor of apprehension. Hunter Reynolds might be a pain in the neck, but he was also a highly educated professional and she likely wasn't much older than some of his students. Customers were always telling her she looked young to be running her own business.

She leaned forward for a quick check in the rear-view mirror: hair curving below prominent cheek-bones, well cut and shiny, makeup confined to a touch of eye shadow and lip gloss. She'd decided against casual wear and gone with her normal workday outfit of navy blazer, white blouse, and gray skirt. Bad enough that Hunter Reynolds had a low opinion of her agency—she was not about to give him a chance to fault her on her professional appearance.

A gust of music blew out to meet her as she mounted the stone step between twin geranium trees. She had to ring the bell twice and was about to try for a third time when the oak door swung open and she found herself staring up at a big golden bear of a man. Friendly brown eyes that must have absorbed some of the morning's sun met hers head-on.

"Hi. Can I help you?"

Not old enough to be the professor, she decided. Nothing at all like the curmudgeon on the telephone. She registered whittled-down hips in light cotton slacks and broad sloping shoulders under a fawn pull-over with the sleeves pushed up to reveal tanned, mus-cular forearms.

"Marchmaids. The cleaning service? Professor Reynolds is—"

"I'm Hunter Reynolds." His gaze took in the marching maid logo on her blazer pocket, shifted to the carryall bag in her hand, and roamed upward over the rest of her at a leisurely pace before settling on her face. "Well, well! Seems neither of us is any great shakes at forming visual impressions over the phone," he said. "Come in, won't you?"

He stepped aside to let her pass and she noticed that his feet were bare, the toes pink and damp and astonishingly attractive. She tore her glance away. The fragrance of some woodsy soap or other hung in the air, embarrassingly intimate.

"I suppose you were expecting an older woman?" she said stiffly.

"I've just come from the shower," he explained. "As a matter of fact, I'd been thinking of somebody alone the lines of my fifth grade math teacher. And you?"

"Since we're being frank—" She paused; she was having a hard time recalling the image she'd invested with all those unpleasant features. "I thought biologists-turned-professor were . . . well, more—that is . . ." The words died in her throat. How was she going to get herself out of this without sounding rude?

He grinned, reinforcing the impression of boyish good looks.

"Dried-up?" he said helpfully. "Skinny? Cantankerous old goats in wire-rim spectacles and hiking boots? Absentminded, too—but there you may be right." His eyes flashed so engagingly with laughter that when he held out his big square paw of a hand, she felt obliged to shake it. His grip was firm and faintly moist from the shower and left a fresh tingling sensation on her palm.

"Seems we'll both have to make do with what we see, Ms. Briarwood."

"I was going to say, more mature," she muttered. But he wasn't about to let her off easily.

"Depends on what you had in mind. I'm thirty-four. Mature enough for most things."

Warmth flooded her cheeks, a sensation she hadn't

experienced in years. Something in the way he looked at her as he said it. As though he didn't mind in the least that she hadn't turned out to resemble his math teacher. This, she reminded herself, was the same Hunter Reynolds who kept chipmunks in a showcase home, practiced blackmail over the phone, and had lost Marchmaids two cleaners in a single Saturday.

"I certainly hope so," she said pointedly. "Before we have that talk you agreed to yesterday, why don't I take care of the mess in the kitchen? I'm sure we both want to get this over with as quickly as possible."

"You'd be right there." He fell into step beside her. "You have other plans for today? An outing with a friend?"

As if he cared! "No outing," she told him coolly. "Only laundry and taking inventory." In the atrium the fountain leaped and dazzled. The ferns and purple gloxinia banked around the rim were holding up well so far, she was relieved to note. She wished she weren't so conscious of his bare feet keeping time with hers on the marble tiles.

"You don't have to come with me. I know the way," she said, and winced as a clash of cymbals reverberated overhead. Kettledrums rumbled. A thunderstorm appeared to be building in the high airy spaces under the skylight. She could almost see the dust motes colliding in front of Rene's speakers.

"Do you always play your music so loudly?" she yelled.

"It's a big house. Takes a big sound to fill. Don't you care for Ludwig?"

Beethoven, she supposed he meant. She bit back a retort about being too busy earning a living to be on a first-name basis with the composers. Margaret had been after her for years to take a break, attend a concert sometime, and find out what she was missing. They were passing through the formal living room now and she kept her eyes open for telltale signs of hard living.

It was such a lovely room—all rosewood and gleaming glass on yards of cream carpeting. A rosy floral fabric bloomed on wingback chairs and swathed floor-to-ceiling windows. The walls were hung with Belgian tapestries, and shelves displayed the centuries-old porcelain and Venetian glass that were Margaret's pride and joy. Facing each other across the carved fireplace were a pair of matching sofas in cream watered silk. March slowed her step.

"Is that *ink* on the cushions?" She sounded as horrified as she felt but it was wasted on him.

"So it is! I was marking papers on the sofa last night. Must have dozed off."

He flicked a button in a panel on the wall and the thunder rolled away on the horizon. March sailed ahead, stifling a comment about people who knew their way around electronic wizardry but were incapable of controlling a ballpoint pen.

In the doorway of The Cedars' state-of-the-art kitchen she couldn't help herself—she gasped out loud.

"How many chipmunks did you say?"

"Four." He had the grace to look apologetic. "I made a stab at cleaning up myself."

"Hmm." She could see where he'd dragged the vacuum cleaner hose through drifts of flour and sugar, clearing a wavy path. Cereal flakes crunched underfoot as she approached the table, and underneath, like a tide-swept island, lay the shredded remains of a corn-flakes box.

"Something got in the pipe so I had to stop."

She thumped down her bag, shrugged off her blazer, and tied on her work apron. "And where are the culprits now?"

"Don't worry. Safe in the solarium, locked up in their cage. Speaking of which," he said with an off-hand wave, "you were right. Your cleaners didn't open the cage—the chipmunks did. I caught one of them at it while I was eating breakfast in there this morning. Amazing! I had no idea their IQs were up to problem-solving of that magnitude."

Deplorable was what it was, not amazing. "Are you suggesting this could be a regular occurrence? Because if it is—"

"Heck no! Not if I can help it. I've wired the latch shut."

She nodded. She'd have more to say to him later. Right now she was itching to get started with the cleanup. Flour lay in a mist over the countertops. Sticky pink paw prints danced from an open jar of raspberry jam up and down the toaster and the coffee-maker and fingered Margaret's black-and-white designer cannisters looking for a way in. More prints trekked through the sink and onto the glass cooktop, leaving behind lumps of paste that stuck like barnacles. March rooted in her bag for heavy artillery.

"I tried detergent," Hunter Reynolds said over her shoulder, making her nerve ends jump. "I even tried scraping the stuff off with a knife."

"So I see." In the process he'd scored a couple of grooves here and there. "It's too late to do anything about those, but industrial-strength cleaner should take care of the prints.''

''Impressive!''

He lounged against the counter, large and very much in the way. Impossible to ignore. ''Obviously what I need around here is a live-in Marchmaid.''

She'd heard that line before. In nine years of cleaning, there weren't many she hadn't heard. All the same, his tone made her feel light-headed in a way she wouldn't have expected. ''I'll leave you the can,'' she said crisply.

''It's still only second best,'' he said, joking.

''That's all you'll get,'' she said. From her, anyway. She frowned at the jammy trail leading up the net curtains and in one swift movement slid them off the rod and piled them in his arms.

''Put those in the laundry room, will you, and the team can wash them next Saturday.''

It gave him something to do, she thought, and in the relief of having him gone, she paused for a moment to dream out the window at the swimming pool sparkling in the sun. White chairs beckoned from under the umbrella and late-blooming sedum glowed like candle flame against the dark backdrop of the cedar hedge.

''I'm sure Margaret has a bathing suit you could borrow,'' he murmured, back again on silent soles and shamelessly reading her mind.

''Blocked, did you say?'' she asked, turning in her brisk way. She picked up the vacuum cleaner hose and energetically pried the metal pipes apart. Wadded into the final joint was the cereal box liner. ''Good as new,'' she declared, extracting it and fitting the pipes back together. "Are you going to stand around watching me all morning?"

"Frankly, I'm intrigued." This time his grin revealed a heart-stopping dimple in his chin. He was rattling her composure and he knew it. "I've never seen anybody attack cleaning with such verve."

"You must have work of your own to do," she persisted. "Lectures to prepare, papers to mark, or whatever it is professors do." She gave him one of Margaret's sharp looks. "But not with a pen on my sister's sofas." She thrust the end of the hose into the wall outlet before he could respond, and listened for the hushed roar of the motor in the basement. Now she felt more in command of herself.

"You could put shoes on for a start," she said, raising her voice. "Your bare feet are tracking sugar all through the house."

"Is that that tickling sensation I've noticed?" He laughed the deep easygoing laugh that had so annoyed her over the phone and disappeared, taking the sound with him.

Perversely, she wished he hadn't.

After she'd mopped the floor, she cleaned the interior of the cabinets, jotting down a list of grocery staples he'd need to replace as she went along. A man hopeless at cleaning probably wasn't much better at shopping. She worked fast and ended by giving the room a tour of inspection. On an impulse, she looked into the dishwasher. It was full of Margaret's wedding china.

March picked out a dinner plate worth half a week's wages, and ran shocked fingers over the fluted blue-and-white rim crusted with mustard. Or was that grilled cheese? He'd been accumulating the dishes for days, she thought, and transferred them to the sink to wash by hand. The anger that had cooled when she met him face-to-face was coming to a boil again. Two of the place settings had been a wedding gift from her, purchased with money she'd earned scrubbing office floors at night.

She found him in Rene's study, sprawled on the leather settee, reading. His hair, spiky from the shower when she'd first seen him, had dried to an unruly halo the color of honey and the pink toes were decently concealed in tennis shoes. The shoes were resting on top of the coffee table. March sighed and wiped damp hands on her apron.

He looked up from his book. "Fire away," he said comfortably.

"Those legs aren't very strong," she observed.

"They're not?" He glanced down in surprise at the cotton fabric stretched taut over his muscular thighs.

"I'm talking about the table legs. They're Queen Anne, in case you don't realize."

He groaned and swung his feet to the floor. "How come every last object in this house is either too old or too expensive or too darn breakable to use?"

"Like the Royal Copenhagen, you mean."

"The what?" The grin he'd offered in appeasement faded. "You look pale. Don't tell me! More problems in the kitchen?"

"Only that you've been using Margaret's best china. Eating grilled cheese and mustard off it and putting it in the dishwasher where the scouring action damages the fluting and the detergent fades the pattern . . ." Her voice, just nicely gathering steam, faltered as he stood up, six feet two of startled disbelief looming over her.

"I don't eat mustard off plates. I eat it off hot dogs. Are you telling me that in a house equipped with the latest in technological marvels, I should be washing dishes by hand?"

"Yes. If it's the fine china," she said stubbornly. Now that she'd provoked him she might as well go all the way. "Which I'm sure Margaret didn't intend you to use anyway." His frown was growing in intensity and she hastened to come to the point. "At least not every day. That's what the kitchen set of dishes is for. The Royal Copenhagen is for special occasions only—"

His eyes narrowed. "Like tonight. For the dean and his wife."

"Exactly," she said, relieved he was being cooperative.

The twitch at the corner of his expressive mouth should have alerted her. "Actually, I was planning a barbecue tonight." At the sight of her face the twitch became a grin. "Relax, Ms. Briarwood. Barbecued hamburgers wouldn't taste right on anything but paper plates. It's an ambience thing."

"Like having chipmunks and students in the house?" she shot back.

Laying down ground rules was going to be more complicated than she'd anticipated. The papers littering the room were none of her business but there was a soccer ball under the desk and somebody had been having fun with the African wood carvings in Rene's bookcase. Frowning, she righted a flamingo being trampled by a giraffe. It was just a matter of time before breakage occured, big time.

"Last I heard, there was a law against keeping wild animals confined."

"Not if they're too young to fend for themselves."

"I suppose you're going to tell me the same goes for university students."

Their glances locked. Storm clouds had swallowed up the sunshine in the brown eyes. "Have you any idea, Ms. Briarwood, how lonely it gets for out-of-town students away from home for the first time?"

"I'm afraid not. I never went to college myself." She gave him a dark look of her own. The admission still rankled, even at twenty-seven. "There is one thing I hope we can be clear about. I do not want my staff subjected to any more episodes like yesterday's."

"Don't worry. I've read those chipmunks the riot act. There'll be no more prison breaks." His expression mellowed. "Have you ever seen *Tamias striatus* up close?" She felt his light touch on her shoulder. "Come on. You can check the security arrangements for yourself while you're at it."

The bougainvillea was in crimson bloom all the way up to the curved glass roof of the solarium. March loved this room, where the light came filtered through leaves. She breathed in the scent of orange blossoms and felt the knot of tension in her stomach loosen. Shade-dwelling azaleas and caladmium sheltered under the sloping branches of a Norfolk Island pine, and in a sunny corner, bromeliads and crown-of-thorn bloomed year-round. Drawn up on the slate floor around a table were cane chairs heaped with print cushions in shades of teal and old rose.

"Behind the pine," said Hunt Reynolds. She looked and there was the cage, roomily constructed of wood and fitted on one side with wire mesh. Inside she glimpsed a driftwood branch and a length of hollow log nestled in a carpet of moss.

"Nice. Like a bit of forest," she said, bending closer. She had the feeling he was crowding her, even though he was only standing there, and it seemed to restrict her breathing. "Where are the tenants?"

He laughed and unhooked the latch. "Don't sound so suspicious. They're asleep in the log."

His big hand, surprisingly deft, reached inside and drew out a glossy brown ball of fur. A white stripe edged in black and tan traced the curving spine; the nose was tucked into the soft whisk tail. The animal opened sleepy eyes, yawned, and sat up in Hunt Reynolds's palm. March experienced a rush of tender, protective feeling.

"I had no idea they were so small!" Considering the domestic havoc they'd wreaked. "Where did they come from?"

"A conscience-stricken cat owner dropped them off at the zoology lab. Orphans, apparently. As soon as they're old enough, I'll find them some woods to live in. Watch."

He held out a sunflower seed. Gravely the chipmunk clasped it in tiny forepaws, jaws working in speeded-up motion as it ate. March glanced at the face of the man and the tender feeling expanded in spite of her. Big bear that he was, Hunter Reynolds was also a pushover for a pint-sized rodent with shoe-button eyes and a fancy overcoat.

"Want to hold him?"

She thought of Cheryl. "He won't bite?"

"Trust me," he said, and something in his face and tone made it easy to do. "Here. Like this."

He turned her hand palm upward and tipped the chipmunk lightly into it. Startled, she smiled. The weight couldn't be more than a few ounces. Hunter

Reynolds smiled back, straight into her eyes, as he handed her a seed, and the smile felt a lot more hazardous than the needle prick of the grasping paws as she passed it on. A lot more penetrating, too. Uneasily she felt herself respond in some deep, hidden place inside her heart.

Margaret was right, she thought—he had charm. The kind she wanted to stay well away from. "Does he have a name?" she blurted out. Anything to keep the conversation on an impersonal level.

He shrugged. "Biologists aren't into anthropomorphy as a rule. I think of them as One, Two, Three, and Four. This is One—the largest. Also the ringleader, aren't you, big guy?"

March watched as he deposited him back in the cage. By now the others had awakened and were chasing each other up and down the driftwood branch.

"You've made your point, Professor Reynolds," she said. "They're lovable creatures and probably harmless enough. All the same . . ."

"Tell you what. If you drop the professor and call me Hunt, on Monday I'll buy a combination lock." His eyes teased. "Electric fencing, too, and maybe a moat?"

"The lock will do," she said. Although some kind of fencing around his eyes—his whole person—might be an idea. "I hate to bring up the subject again, but isn't that the Royal Copenhagen sugar bowl?"

"This?" He reached for the sunflower seed dish and groaned. "We'll go and change it right now."

In the kitchen he let out a whistle of admiration. "You sure know how to make a man feel humble!"

She was pleased in spite of herself, but embarrassed, too. "You're forgetting, it's my job."

"Don't kid yourself. I'm not forgetting anything about you," he countered. She tucked her apron into the carryall and pretended not to notice the flattering gleam in his eye. "Good. I hope that includes my concerns about the house." She plucked her blazer from the chair. "I've left a list of groceries you'll need to buy. And now, if you'll give me my check, Professor Reynolds, I'll be on my way."

"Hunt," he repeated, walking her to the door. From a pocket he produced an envelope with her name written on it in Margaret's elegant script. "You might as well have the whole caboodle. I don't foresee any reason to withhold them in the future. Do you?"

"Not on Marchmaids' part, I don't."

He chuckled. "You stick to your guns, don't you? I like that in a woman. Would it help make up for what happened if I asked you to the barbecue?"

"Really, there's—"

"Bring somebody along if you like. A friend or whatever," he added, to forestall the "no" he saw forming on her face.

"Thanks. There is no friend or whatever." She laughed and set him straight. *Do it now,* she thought. Before she weakened and it was too late. "You might as well know, it's against Marchmaids' policy for staff to socialize with customers. It's apt to lead to—well, complications, you understand."

He leaned an arm against the doorjamb, effectively barring her exit. "Does this apply to the company CEO, as well?"

Especially to the CEO, thought March with the tinge of bitterness reminders of Kent Harrison invariably engendered. "I wouldn't ask anything of my staff that I wouldn't ask of myself."

"Ah." He digested this. "Such as working on Sundays. But you do indulge in pleasure the odd time?" he asked innocently. "In between the demands of importunate clients and, what was it you said—laundry and inventory?"

"Every day," she said, matching his tone. "It might surprise you to know, I'm one of those rare fortunate people who enjoy their work."

He lifted an amused tawny eyebrow. "I could always put tonight's invitation on a business footing. Ask you to keep an eye on the Vermeer treasures. Make sure none of the guests wander onto the carpets with those flimsy paper plates. Or leave can rings on the Queen Anne."

"Heaven forbid!"

He wasn't serious, was he? She hesitated. But that was crazy—she couldn't baby-sit the house every time he had people in to visit. Even for Margaret's sake.

"Why don't you try the Yellow Pages under Hostess?" she said brightly. "They've got services to cover every need nowadays."

She pushed past him, using her bag to run interference. "Good-bye, Professor . . . Hunt," she amended, with a tilt of her chin.

"Good-bye, March."

His eyes followed her out to the car. She could feel them, warmer than the midday sun between her shoulder blades. As she stowed her carryall in the hatch, he called out, "I'll put an extra hamburger on the grill. Just in case you change your mind."

She climbed in behind the wheel. "Suit yourself," she said, and reached for the door to slam it shut. "But I won't!"

Which was really too bad, she thought as she turned into Parkway Drive for the drive home. Because for the first time since she'd broken up with Kent, she would very much have liked to.

Chapter Three

They were like a troop of magicians ready to perform the day's magic. March smiled at the fanciful thought. Clipboard in hand, she watched the cleaning teams finish loading equipment into their cars.

The sun was clearing the rooftops and the morning breeze ruffling her hair felt light and clean after last night's rain. A teeming downpour that had left puddles in the driveway, it was certain to have put a damper on Hunt Reynolds's barbecue. With any luck, he'd canceled the whole affair and she'd worried about Margaret's possessions for nothing.

"Ever notice," she remarked, closing the door on what promised to be a sensational fall day, "how things look best in the early morning?"

"Before they start falling apart, you mean." Anna Rose glanced up from the kitchen sink with a smile. Fresh from her Sunday with Tony, she was her normal placid self again. "Customers canceling. Keys vanishing. Three people wanting rush jobs done on Friday at three."

March laughed. "Yes. I guess that's what I mean."

"So tell me about yesterday." Anna Rose poured coffee for them both into freshly rinsed mugs and seated herself expectantly at the table. "You went over to The Cedars and then what happened?"

"Happened? In what way?" All at once she felt flustered.

"With the professor! The chipmunks! March, is he going to sue us, or are we suing him?"

"Oh, nothing so dramatic." She sipped her coffee. "It turned out to be a pretty civilized encounter, really. He admitted the chipmunks getting out wasn't our fault, and I agreed to clean up. Seems he'd invited some VIP guests for dinner last night so he was up the creek."

"And that's it?"

"Basically." Except for the fact that he'd invited her as well, but why bother to mention that when she hadn't accepted? "Lucky I went. He had the dishwasher full of Royal Copenhagen."

"That bad! What about giving students the run of the house? Did you get him to promise to stop?"

"Not exactly." How could she explain? Hunter Reynolds wasn't the type of man who could be made to stop anything he wanted to do. "He's not at all the way we expected . . ." She hesitated, the flustered feeling returning as Anna Rose narrowed thoughtful eyes across the table.

"You mean he's not pushing sixty and didn't brandish a paddle?"

"I did say that, didn't I?" March marveled, grinning, and laced slender fingers around her mug.

"Try thirty-four. With blond hair you want to run your fingers through and shoulders like a bear. He drives a Range Rover and plays Beethoven as though it were heavy metal. And when he held one of the chipmunks, you could see he really cares . . ." She raised her head, aware that her companion's lips had parted in astonishment.

"It just goes to show, doesn't it, you never can tell about people over the phone," she finished lamely.

"Doesn't it just! Next you'll have me believing the chipmunks were kind of cute, too." Anna Rose reached for their empty mugs and March wasn't sure she liked the expression on her face.

"They were, as a matter of fact. And don't start getting ideas!"

"I wouldn't dream of it. But you seem to have a few already."

The conversation was getting out of hand and she was going to have to stop it right here. "Anna Rose! Even if I did, you know how I feel about Marchmaids and male customers."

"So you should. It's *your* policy." Anna Rose glanced at the clock and relented. "Well, I'm on my way. I've got inspections this morning. Want me to drop off that Help Wanted ad?"

"No, thanks anyway. I'll be driving right by the Employment Center." Monday was her day to pick up supplies at the wholesaler's. "Anything we need that you can think of?"

"Oven cleaner, but you've got that on the list already." Anna Rose rummaged in her bag for car keys. "I notice you left out 'must be hardworking' this time."

"It only scares applicants off. We need somebody yesterday. Which reminds me, it might be a good idea if the two of us did the cleaning at The Cedars for a week or two."

"If you say so." Anna Rose turned at the door with an infuriating smile. "He's not married, this Hunter Reynolds, is he?" she said.

"Are you leaving or do I have to fire you?" exclaimed March.

But it didn't help. The smile returned full force to mind a couple of hours later, when March pulled into her driveway and discovered the Range Rover parked in her spot.

Even more annoying was the sudden attack of breathlessness that occurred as the driver's door opened and a pair of long legs encased in tan corduroy emerged, followed by the rest of Hunt Reynolds in a leather bomber jacket the color of cognac. A man shouldn't be allowed to look that good. Especially when his presence could mean only one thing—trouble.

"Hi!"

His easy stride brought him over to where she stood warily, keys in hand. "I was just about to give up and go home."

Against her will, she found herself matching his smile. "Good morning, Professor. Is there something I can do for you?"

"Hunt. You missed a great barbecue last night."

"Did I?" She raised the hatch to hide an unexpected pang. "I was hoping you might have canceled it because of the rain."

He laughed his warm, self-assured laugh. His hair had a spun-gold look in the sun. "It takes more than rain to stop a Reynolds barbecue. May I lift that for you?" he said, as she reached for the oven cleaner. Hoisting the case under one arm, he scooped up a jug of wax stripper and two carrier bags in the other. "Got the house key?" he enquired pleasantly.

"Really, I can carry my own—" She bit off the ungracious protest and unlocked the door. "Through there and to your left,'' she said, pointing. What did he mean, it took more than rain? Where exactly had he held the barbecue? She was afraid to ask.

"On the floor?'' he suggested, and she nodded.

"I'll restock the shelves later.''

He straightened up and the narrow supply room shrank another couple of feet. "Smells good in here. Like lemon and fresh ironing,'' he commented, his interested gaze taking in the assortment of cans and bottles, the bin full of clean rags, the wire-mesh baskets brimming with clean folded aprons. Light from the window silhouetted his shoulders and tapering mid-section and made a deceptive halo of his hair as he turned to smile at March. "A bit like you, in fact.''

If he thought that was flattering, he was wrong. "I'm a busy woman, Professor. I imagine you're here for a reason?''

"That's like you, too. A man pays you a compliment and you think he wants something cleaned.'' He shook his head, smiling to take the sting out of his assessment. "Unfortunately, in this case you'd be right. I was hoping you could let me have some carpet shampoo. I noticed one or two stains this morning.''

Abruptly she stopped focusing on his smile. "What kind of stains?''

"Wine stains. Red wine,'' he specified helpfully. "In the living room.''

March groaned inwardly. Did people ever spill white wine on cream carpeting? Not to her knowledge. "You actually served wine—with hamburgers—''

"A bit gauche, you think?''

"—in the living room?'' she finished on a rising note. He certainly knew how to make her see red. Wine red, as it happened, only this wasn't a joke. "I can't believe it! In spite of the talk we had, you went ahead and let your guests eat and drink in a room that's been featured in *Home Decorating*?''

''What did you want me to do?'' He looked defensive. ''Leave them out on the patio when the heavens opened up? It was tricky enough trying to barbecue under Rene's golf umbrella.''

''I don't know! You could have insisted they stick to the kitchen! The solarium! You—'' She stopped; she was trembling all over. Actually, the thought of him under the umbrella was rather funny. Not that she'd do him the favor of admitting it. ''Sorry. It's none of my business, is it? How you do your entertaining.''

''To be honest, no.''

Chagrined, she fumbled a tin off the shelf. ''Rug shampoo,'' she muttered, thrusting it in his hands. ''It won't remove the whole stain, but it'll be a start and we can work on the rest with the steamer. Was there any other''—she had to force herself to say the word—''damage?''

He shrugged and she wondered why it was that the bigger the man, the more helpless he looked when he got into trouble.

''Since you mention it, somebody left a hot dog on the arm of a wingback chair. Mustard and relish, I believe. But we're lucky—it hardly shows against the pattern.''

She closed her eyes briefly, then grabbed some more tins. ''Spot removers. If one doesn't do the trick, the other might. Only for heaven's sake, read the instructions first.'' She watched him stuff the tins in his jacket pocket. ''Maybe I should come over myself and—''

He held up his hand. "Not this time. I appreciate the offer, March, but you're making too big a deal of this. Life is for living. Chairs are for sitting in, carpets for catching what falls. Even at The Cedars. Okay?" He grinned, sure of himself again, and placing light fingers above her elbow, propelled her out of the room.

Her arm tingled as though she'd come in contact with an electrical outlet. "Easy for you to say. I'm the one responsible—"

"You work too hard," he said firmly. "Six days a week and Sundays if your customers are thoughtless enough to demand it. Sure, you enjoy your work, but work's not all there is to life. Thanks for the assist and I'll be out of your way now. Class in twenty minutes," he explained, opening the door while she was still trying to formulate a response. On the step, he pivoted.

"I nearly forgot. That vase on top of the credenza? I suppose it's authentic."

A cold hand clutched at her stomach. "Authentic Ming dynasty, according to Margaret. Why? What happened to it?"

"No need to shout. It didn't break. There's something to be said for expensive carpeting."

She stared at him. She was all out of words.

"Apparently it's one of those laws of physics? The music and the dancing set up a vibration that caused the vase to inch forward and topple over the edge. Ted Lawrence, in Science, knew all about it."

She had been naive, thought March weakly. Worrying about mere china and carpets, when irreplaceable art objects were at risk.

"I don't suppose you were playing Beethoven," she said, in a grim attempt at humor.

"Heck no. Dire Straits, as I recall."

Dire Straits! It must have been quite a party.

After he'd left, she went in the kitchen to fortify herself with a sandwich and a cup of tea but they didn't seem to fill the emptiness inside. The aching sense that life was passing her by. The last real party she'd attended had been with Kent, a New Year's dance held in the ballroom of the Weatherfield Arms. There'd been lobster and champagne, and a live band with a surprisingly up-to-date repertoire. Only every time they played anything livelier than a fox-trot, Kent insisted they sit the piece out. Because his boss and the board of directors were attending as well, and he didn't want them to get the wrong idea. Bad enough, he said, that March had shown up in a silver lamé dress, and wasn't that hemline a bit short? She'd passed the dress on to Cheryl afterward, but she had never felt the same about going out with Kent.

She was changing from her skirt and blouse after lunch, when the Employment Center rang.

They were sending over an applicant for the job at 4:15. March glanced at her watch. Giving Agnes Rowland's cherrywood dining suite its annual polishing would take her the best part of the afternoon. It was a job she'd previously left to Liz, who was a whiz at antiques. Moodily, she scribbled instructions for Anna Rose to do the interview in her place. Another complication for which she could thank Hunt Reynolds! The man was as pervasive as air freshener and even less useful.

"I think she applied because of the uniform," observed Anna Rose, as the door closed behind a young woman in a miniskirt. "Cute, she called it."

March rubbed a stained hand over the nape of her neck. "If she only knew!" She'd walked in just as Anna Rose trotted out the standard line that they'd let her know after they'd interviewed the other applicants.

"I'm beat. I swear the vine leaves on the buffet have multiplied. Never mind. Those other applicants are bound to show up eventually."

"You hope." Grumbling, Anna Rose crossed to the change room. "Look at this place! The times I've told them! Aprons in the bin."

"Go home. Would you please? It's after five and all I want is a shower and something to eat I can get on the table in ten minutes flat."

Anna Rose's face grew dreamy as she thrust her arms into her jacket. "Tony said he'd get supper started tonight. We're going to watch a romantic comedy on video tonight. Just the two of us, at home." Her brow arched. "Doesn't that give you any ideas?"

"Yes! To go out and buy myself a microwave and a VCR. Have a nice evening, you two lovebirds!"

She didn't need Anna Rose's comments to give her ideas, March thought, pushing one weary leg ahead of the other up the flight of stairs to her private retreat under the eaves. She'd been having them herself lately, for the first time since her breakup with Kent. Ideas regarding someone male to come home to at the end of the day. Not that Kent had cared much for domesticity, she recalled, her gaze lost in the gold of the maple through her dormer window.

He preferred going out. Spending an evening with her busy in the kitchen reminded him too much that she cleaned houses for a living. He hadn't been big on sofa scenes either, even in his own apartment, furnished in masculine style with lots of glass and leather on the seventeenth floor of a downtown high-rise. Kissing, undeniably pleasant because he'd been a good-looking man in his sober, button-down fashion— that was as far as they'd gone.

Protesting muscles called her back to the present.

She unzipped her navy jumpsuit and peeled off her clothes, her movements reflected in graceful gleams of ivory in her mother's cheval glass. In the adjoining bathroom, she clapped the shower panel shut and gave herself up to the luxury of steaming water. The problem with nineteenth-century furniture was that it had been designed by men. A woman would have foreseen the hours of maintenance work ahead and gone easy on the vines and roses. Why was it men so often had trouble with the practical? Take Hunt Reynolds!

March drizzled shampoo on her hair and lathered up a blizzard. Smart enough to survive the wilds, not to mention a classroom full of university students, he seemed unable to keep a million-dollar home from deteriorating around him.

She had thought about him a lot this afternoon. He was no Kent Harrison. Her mind seemed only too eager to dwell on the dazzle of his hair in the sun, the amused intelligent spark in his eyes, the way his big male body gave off simultaneous signals of gentleness and power . . . A little involuntary shiver ran through her as she rinsed her hair.

"Oh, for heaven's sake," she muttered, mortified at the direction her thoughts were taking. She'd have to keep her mind on business.

It was Wednesday before she found the right applicant for their vacant position. Anna Rose wasn't so sure.

"But Jamie Douglas is a man!"

"So?" March scraped boiled-over milk off the top of Freda Walmsley's stove, and aimed a resentful thought at the man to blame. All week she'd been forced to fill in for missing staff.

"A male Marchmaid? Customers may not be comfortable with that."

She pushed the hair back from her forehead with her arm. For somebody only two years older than she was, Anna Rose could be awfully old-fashioned. "Why should they care? As long as he does the job. He's available and his references check out. Besides—" She shrugged. "There is such a thing as equal employment."

Anna Rose frowned at the burner pans she was scouring. "You think the staff will accept him? He's pretty young . . ."

"Twenty. The same age as Andrea." March wiped the enamel to a sparkling finish. "Why don't we ask them? Call a meeting and see if anybody objects."

"I suppose," conceded Anna Rose, drying her hands. "Well, I've done my best. It's a wonder there's any finish left on these pans."

"They're getting old. Like Freda."

"But who else still leaves tea and cookies for their cleaners?"

She plugged in the kettle while March stowed away their cleaning things. Freda had been her first customer. Over the years the flowered china cups and the digestive biscuits hadn't changed. Neither had the old house with its outdated appliances. Wobbly-legged tables overflowed with mementos, and framed photographs recording the Walmsley nieces and nephews in a succession of christenings, graduations, and weddings made dusting a major undertaking.

At least Freda had a family—unlike Hunt Reynolds. Although he must have had one to start with; everybody did, even nomads more at home with wildlife. No matter that she hadn't laid eyes on the man for days—she couldn't seem to stop finding grounds to wonder about him. Freda's tomcat drifted into the kitchen in time for the biscuits and wove his purring, furry self around their legs.

"That's another advantage of hiring Jamie. He grew up on a farm, so he's used to animals. Like chipmunks."

"Chipmunks are not farm animals," Anna Rose said pointedly.

March sighed and they sipped their tea in silence. "Hunt Reynolds hasn't called lately, has he?" she asked, losing an interior battle against bringing up his name.

"No. Was there a particular reason he should?"

She hadn't mentioned his visit Monday. Gleeful insinuations from Anna Rose were the last thing she needed! Gratitude was too much to ask of Hunt, she supposed, but yes, she had expected him to call. If only to let her know whether the stains had come out.

"No reason," she said. "No news is good news, from The Cedars." The phrase sounded forlorn. *Well, why wouldn't it?* she thought darkly. They'd probably find all all kinds of unpleasant surprises waiting for them Saturday.

The staff meeting the next morning went well— better even than she'd anticipated.

"If the guy pulls his weight, why not?" declared Bettina, who had grown up with three brothers and regarded the male sex with friendly scorn. "The extra muscle might come in handy for wrestling fridges off the wall."

"If he's cute, I'd be glad to move the fridge for him," said Andrea wistfully. Big-boned and handsomely freckled, she was perennially on the lookout for boyfriends. But how would he look in the March-maids apron? Joan wanted to know, and everybody laughed. When March asked for a show of hands, they all voted in favor of giving Jamie a try.

"See? That wasn't so hard," said March, after the teams had left. "Will you call him, or shall I?"

The telephone rang while Anna Rose was looking up his number and she handed March the receiver, eyes dancing. "For you. Speaking of the devil. And I don't mean Jamie."

March was annoyed to feel color flood her cheeks. "Hello?" She held the instrument to her ear as though it were hot metal.

"Busy morning?" asked Hunt Reynolds.

She rolled her eyes; what did he think? "If you really want to know, we're in the process of hiring replacement staff."

"Ouch! I should have seen that coming." His chuckle wasn't in the least embarrassed. "Actually, I'm calling to find out if you'd like a break."

"What kind of break?" Too late, she remembered Anna Rose, her smooth brown head bent over the filing cabinet not five feet away. "Sorry. I don't have time for breaks."

"Tsk, tsk. Forgotten our little talk already?"

"I could ask the same of you."

"Not a word. Everything's cool around here." He paused, and she thought she'd put him off, but no.

"There's a Beethoven concert at Alumni Hall tonight, and I managed to get hold of the last two tickets. Interested?"

She drew a breath. "Sorry, Professor Reynolds. Hunt. I'm afraid you've wasted your money. I did mention, Marchmaids has a policy—"

"—against fraternizing with the enemy. Yes, I know—" The wail of an electric guitar drowned out his voice. "Hold on a sec!" A door slammed and he was back, minus musical accompaniment. "This is not a date I'm asking you on. Heaven forbid! It's strictly to make amends for last weekend. Anyway, concerts don't count. They're serious stuff. You've got to admit, a concert hall is hardly the place for—what did you call them?—complications to develop."

Ten for persuasive argument. March smiled in spite of herself. She *was* tempted. Not by Beethoven, who was a stranger to her, but by the images Hunt's warm, easygoing tones were evoking in her head. All the more reason not to weaken, she told herself. Aloud, she hedged.

"Wasn't that rock music I heard you playing just now?"

He laughed and the images pressed enticingly closer. "Not me. Kim and Chen. That was their boom box you heard."

Kim and Chen? Students, obviously. Her brow tightened. This early in the morning? He didn't elaborate. And he didn't press the invitation, either.

"Some other time, then," he said lightly. "Good luck with the new recruit," he added, and was gone, the dial tone humming, as though her refusal were no big deal.

It probably wasn't, for him. He'd have his choice

of replacements at the university—a big handsome available man like that. And the carpet stains? He hadn't said, and she'd forgotten to ask. She felt suddenly extremely dissatisfied with life.

She wondered if it showed in her face. Anna Rose, reaching for the phone to dial Jamie's number, for once in her life tactfully refrained from comment.

Saturday morning March put away her cereal bowl unused. Her stomach felt jumpy. Apprehension, no doubt, about what they'd find at The Cedars. Or anticipation—which was silly, she told herself firmly, because Hunt would be away at his class. And even if he weren't, she wouldn't be alone with him. Then Joan rang in sick, and Anna Rose arranged to take her place.

"Do you mind? It means you'll have to cope with The Cedars on your own."

"No problem," said March, stifling dismay under a jaunty tone. "I'll leave now. Allow myself extra time."

A mistake, she realized, as soon as she pulled into the brick drive. Hunt was just striding out from behind the house. She felt a cowardly urge to back up, circle the block, and return later. But his wilderness-trained eye had already spotted her through the windshield. He waved, and the sun, which had been struggling with indecision, chose that moment to burst through the clouds.

She felt suddenly, ominously, happy.

"Hi there!" He waited as she climbed out of the car with her carryall. "Are you early this morning, or am I late?"

"I thought I'd get an early start. Since I'm on my

own today.'' The breeze ran loving fingers through his hair. He was wearing custom-fitted fawn trousers and a brown tweed jacket over an oatmeal turtleneck. March swallowed. She had no idea wildlife biologists looked so sharp in their lecturing clothes. ''We're still one cleaner short,'' she added, pulling herself together.

He gave her a shrewd look. ''So the CEO has to pitch in.''

''That's right.''

It wouldn't hurt him to realize it. She turned to lift out the rest of her equipment and he sauntered over to help.

''Haven't I seen this contraption before?''

''It's the carpet steamer,'' she informed him as he swung it onto the bricks. One hint of his woodsy after-shave and already she felt intoxicated. ''You didn't say whether the wine stains came out.''

''Almost.''

Their eyes met and she had the most extraordinary sensation of being drawn into a swirling, amber pool. Lured by something she glimpsed in the depths and wanted desperately to see more of.

''But I got the mustard off the wingback,'' he was saying. His breathing sounded a bit ragged but no doubt that was her imagination. ''The chipmunks haven't cracked the combination on the lock, and nobody's touched the china. Three out of four isn't bad, is it?''

''No.'' Three out of four was wonderful. More than she'd dared hope for. Staring a man in the eyes like this was stirring up a hornet's nest, she thought helplessly. Especially when he was a customer and not her type at all—

The front door opened. March, released from her

spell, turned to watch in dazed astonishment as two slight young men with bookpacks over their shoulders descended between the geranium trees.

Hunt made the introductions.

"March Briarwood. Kim and Chen Li. I believe I mentioned them over the phone? They're brothers from China, taking my class, and their English is still a bit shaky," he added, as they smiled politely. One of them, taller and thinner than the other, inclined his head in a bow that made his straight black hair flop over the rim of his glasses.

"They're . . . living with you? Here in the house?" She gave them a strained smile back. "Since when?"

"Since Tuesday. When I found out they were sharing a one-bedroom apartment with five other people. Being charged an outrageous rent and with barely enough funds left to feed themselves."

March frowned and dropped her gaze. Sad, naturally, and none of her business if Hunt chose to give some students a home. But the consequences could be. "You do realize that The Cedars isn't just any ordinary house. The Vermeers' art collection . . ."

Hunt's expression cooled. "The Chinese have been living in houses a lot longer than most of us. Creating art we in the West—"

"I know. Like the Ming vase," she fired back, and he made a sound of disgust. Heat rose to her face but she stood her ground. The young men had wandered over to the garage—out of earshot, she fervently hoped. "This isn't a frat house. Don't they have parents? Surely the university—"

"The university can do only so much. Do you know when their last money from home came through?" She could tell he was working hard at being patient.

"Five months ago! Are you suggesting I put them out on the street?"

"Not me. I'm thinking of Rene and Margaret— what they would say. Somebody's got to protect their interests."

Hostility vibrated between them. She couldn't believe how quickly the weather had changed. Gone was the friendly bear with melting sunlight in his eyes. This was the bear rampant, the kind you saw on coats of arms rearing up on his hind legs flourishing a bolt of lightning.

"Aren't you rating the Vermeers a trifle low on the social conscience scale? Rene's a friend of mine, too, remember. A good friend."

He had her there.

She frowned into the sun. "But Margaret—" she began, and stopped. Her sister wouldn't thank her for painting her as the heavy in front of a mutual acquaintance. She got a tighter grip on the carryall and steamer. Obviously she'd said all she could about the situation. Mustering her dignity, she started for the house.

"I've got work to do," she said loftily.

"Right." She heard him activate the garage door. "Time and dust wait for no man. Or in this case, maid."

She bit back a retort. There was no need for sarcasm. She struggled into the front hall, hampered by the steamer, which seemed intent on wedging itself against the doorjamb at a combative angle.

Car doors slammed and the Range Rover accelerated down the driveway with the growl of an irate grizzly. Against her will, she glanced back. Just in time to note that Kim and Chen waved good-bye and Hunt, eyes fixed straight ahead, did not.

It shouldn't have mattered to her. But it did.

She knew then she was in trouble. Deep trouble, with more to come if she didn't take steps to get Hunt Reynolds out of her head immediately.

Chapter Four

She doubted Hunt Reynolds would be calling again with invitations to concerts—Beethoven's or anybody else's. Not after the way they'd parted company on Saturday. Even if he did, she certainly hadn't changed her mind about accepting. So why, three days later, was she still making excuses to hang around the telephone and feeling, as she had just now, a rush of anticipation every time it rang?

Disgusted with herself, March bundled her tool kit and the vacuum cleaner whose worn plug she was replacing out of the office and onto the tiled floor of the change room. Anna Rose could take the call. She was the one nearest the phone, filling in time sheets while she waited for her machine.

March snipped through the frayed cord and peeled back the rubber coating to expose the copper wiring inside. It bothered her that she'd come across as so mean-spirited about Hunt's boarders. Giving him the impression that she cared more about the house and its contents than she did about two young lives in need of a helping hand! Impatiently she picked up the new plug, manipulating her pliers as though she could rewire the unfortunate scene. *Red leads to red, blue to blue,* she told herself.

It wasn't as though Kim and Chen had caused any great amount of extra work. Their beds were neatly made, their possessions painfully few. Judging by the printout paper piled in the den, they were taking computer science in addition to Hunt's class. The dishwasher was stacked as before with unwashed dishes— the kitchen set this time. On the table she'd found a trio of wooden salad bowls ingeniously pressed into service as cereal bowls. True to his word, Hunt hadn't touched the Royal Copenhagen.

On an impulse, she left him a note taped to the coffeemaker.

Wouldn't it make sense to invest in a second set of cheap dishes to ease what appeared to be a shortage, now that he had live-in guests? She had signed *Sincerely, March* as a signal that she was trying to be helpful, not judgmental. So far it didn't look as though he'd taken it that way. Tightening the screw, she held up the plug for frowning inspection just as Anna Rose stuck her head in the room.

"That was a Mrs. Golding on the phone. From Warbler Woods? Could we send somebody around this afternoon to do an assessment?"

"Could we!" March scrambled to her feet, putting her gloomy speculations on hold. They had been trying for months to gain a foothold in the luxury subdivision. "I'll go. Here's your vacuum cleaner."

"Thanks. I promised to lend Bettina a hand at the Clendennings. She's got Jamie with her this afternoon. If I'm right, those two are going to make a great team."

"No more doubts about male cleaners, then?"

"Not if they're like Jamie." She grinned from the door. "Good luck with Mrs. Golding. The address is on the telephone pad."

March was tucking the sheet of paper into her bag when the phone rang again.

"March? Hunt here. Glad I caught you. About that note you left me Saturday . . ."

What was it about hearing his voice off guard that made her feel as if she'd come in contact with a high-voltage wire? "Yes?"

"I liked your suggestion. In fact, I'm at the Weatherfield Mall right now, looking at china. But the stuff they're selling strikes me as pretty pricey. Does twenty dollars for something called a fruit nappy sound high to you?"

March gasped. "Exorbitant! Which store is this?"

"That place with the marble columns? They were very nice about letting me use the phone." She heard a woman's throaty laughter.

"You mean Sterling's? 'Sterling's For Fine Wedding China'?" she quoted, aghast. "Eaton's is where you want to go, or The Bay."

"A department store?" He didn't sound enthusiastic. "I should warn you, I've got low staying power when it comes to shopping. Ten minutes wandering through the aisles, and I've been known to grab the nearest item and make a break for Parking. They have some Wedgwood here that looks okay—"

"Buy that and you won't be able to afford to put food on it!" she told him. With her eye on the clock, she made rapid calculations. "Listen, I was just on my way out. If you want some help, I can be there in five minutes."

"I was hoping you'd say that." He chuckled. "First counter on your right."

The receiver clicked in her ear. Obviously there'd been a thaw since their frosty parting. But now what was she getting herself into? All in a good cause—namely the preservation of Margaret's precious Royal Copenhagen. Which hardly explained the surge of excitement lending wings to her steps as she ran to the car.

He was lounging against the counter, very graceful for so large a man, and the focus of attention of not one but three salesclerks. Attractive young women with soigné hairstyles and persuasive voices. She quickened her step.

"Hunt?"

"March!" He sounded relieved. "Sorry, ladies. Some other time," he said, easing their disappointment with a smile. "Am I glad to see you! Another minute and I'd have been reaching for my credit card," he confided under his breath, adjusting his long stride to hers. "Were you aware Wedgwood makes a china service that's dishwasher-proof?"

"Pizza on Wedgwood?" March rolled her eyes ceilingward.

At Eaton's, without pausing to analyze why, she steered him toward the most grandmotherly of the salesclerks and explained what they were looking for. The woman nodded.

"Ironstone. Just the thing. We have a new shipment on display," she said, leading the way.

Hunt rejected a practical floral pattern in favor of seagulls drifting over a blue-and-white background. "I'll take everything you've got—cups, plates, bowls—say a dozen each?"

"No sense buying more than the dishwasher can hold," March pointed out. "How about eight place settings?" He obediently handed over his card and the clerk, her eyes kindly behind her spectacles, asked whether it was their first set of dishes.

"Our—Oh. No!" Hastily March disillusioned her. "This gentleman's first set. He'd like them delivered to 114 Parkway Drive." Out of the corner of her eye she saw Hunt give an ungentlemanly grin.

She pretended to frown. "You know, I've been thinking. About those . . . accidents in the living room. Why not a few scatter rugs, strategically placed? Furniture throws, too—"

"A preemptive strike, so to speak? Sure. If you help select them."

"Well . . ." She remembered Mrs. Golding and glanced at her watch. When he sighed and said, "I suppose I could always go for Aubusson. That's one I know," she knew she was beaten.

She marched him past Aubusson, Rajasthan, and Turkestan, and under her guidance he settled on half a dozen dhurrie mats in serviceable patterns. Across the aisle in Bedspreads & Draperies, they struck it lucky. Woven cotton furniture throws in earth tones guaranteed to blend with every spill were going for a song. While Hunt paid, she inspected linens.

"Soft," he remarked, coming up beside her and poking an experimental fist into a down-filled duvet. "A man could get used to spending the night under one of these things."

She slanted him a glance from beneath her lashes. "Even a man who sleeps in a sleeping bag?"

His eyebrows rose. "How do you know?"

"I cleaned at The Cedars on Saturday, remember?"

"Ah. Could be dangerous. A woman who knows my secrets!" He lowered himself onto the duvet, testing, and laughing up at her with teasing warm eyes.

Did he have to look so relaxed—so at home on that bed? A runaway part of her mind was avidly picturing herself reclining there with him, fitting snugly into the sweater-clad curve of his arm.

"Actually, my bed is more the bedspread type," she informed him, moving primly to the next display.

Hunt caught up with her. "That one," he said. "The one with the scarlet poppies. That's you."

She turned, intrigued. "It is? How can you tell?"

"Easy." He brushed aside the arc of her hair and ran his thumb lightly down the side of her cheek. " 'Poppy bold and bright. With heart as dark as mystery. And skin of petalled light.' " His smile was in his eyes as well as on his lips and she said unsteadily, "That sounds like a poem."

"It is. About a Chinese empress. Who lived five centuries ago and was very much loved." After a silence in which she seemed to be holding her breath, he said, still in the same tone, "Have tea with me? No pagodas in Weatherfield, but I know a place under the trees by the river where they serve rice cakes."

"Really." She shook her head. She felt like someone coming out of a trance. Around them voices resumed talking and people reappeared from a misty limbo into which they'd temporarily vanished. "Hunt. You know I don't—"

"I'm not asking for a date. Heaven forbid! You've helped me out and I'd like to repay you for your time. That's all."

Perversely, she felt a sense of letdown. But he was right; it was only a cup of tea. Why make a big fuss over something that was simply a gesture of appreciation? Next she'd have him thinking that she was reading more into the invitation than he'd put in.

They took the escalator down to the parking garage. Not surprisingly, he'd found a spot directly beside the exit.

"I could follow you in the hatchback," she said, with a last-ditch nod to Mrs. Golding. "To save time." Hunt, opening the door, looked pained. "If we wanted to save time, we'd have stayed in the mall and drunk tea out of Styrofoam in the food court."

The inside of the Range Rover was like a time capsule packed with basic Reynolds information. Snapping her seat belt in place, March took time to glance around. A cassette titled *Wolf Songs* was primed to play, and tucked under the sun visor was a dog-eared map of British Columbia. The backseat offered a sampling of biology texts, raffishly garnished with gym shoes and a tennis racquet. Bumping up against her feet in front was a bag of dog kibble.

Alarmed, she said, "Surely you don't have a—"

"Dog?" The Rover bucketed into the sunshine and he shrugged. "No. Chipmunks like variety in their diet, same as the rest of us."

A sticker on the dashboard proclaimed. HUG AN IN-HABITANT OF EARTH TODAY. *Or share your roof with a few, if you were Hunt Reynolds.* She wouldn't mind being hugged by a man like him, she reflected idly, and immediately sat up straighter. Where had that thought come from? They stopped for lights, the big vehicle grumbling under its breath, and heads turned to look. Women's eyes, March noted, shifted appreciatively to the driver.

"About last Saturday," she began. "I'm sorry if I gave the wrong impression. Kim and Chen seemed like very nice boys."

His gaze brushed hers. "And a lot neater than you expected."

"That too," she admitted. He didn't hold grudges, but he stood up for what he knew was right. Fair enough. Late roses bloomed in a park, reminding her that she should be indoors working. "How much farther, to this place you're taking us?" she wanted to know.

"Relax. This is it."

The Riverview Café stood at the end of a paved drive, a low white building topped with a railing and arched with wide windows in a style that made her think of old-fashioned dance pavilions. Marigolds blazed around a fountain, and tall trees in autumn dress stepped leisurely down to the river.

"The terrace?" he prompted, and she nodded, aware suddenly that it was a day in a million and she was happy.

They sat under a yellow-and-white umbrella. Dusty millers silvered the bank, spangled with blue lobelias, and the water reflected the trees in smooth-flowing bands of copper and gold. March sighed with the sheer pleasure of it all, and lifted her face to the sun.

"Two pots of jasmine tea," Hunt told the waiter. "And make that a double order of rice cakes. We've been shopping."

She laughed. "Which you did very well, for a man who's mall-shy."

"Thanks to you." He raised a wry brow. "I guess it's no secret that I'm out of my depths at The Cedars. I'm not into possessions myself. Not like Rene. It's the old business of the rolling stone . . ."

"Gathering no moss? Tell me about it—I've never met one before." She leaned her chin on her hand and gazed across the table. "How does it start? That kind of life?"

"In my case it came with the job. I did fieldwork for the government. Studying wolves in the Arctic. Marmots in the Rockies. For a while I was overseas on an exchange program. A game preserve in Kenya."

She listened to his anecdotes, enchanted. She could see why he'd had to bring home those chipmunks. Margaret was lucky Weatherfield didn't run to lions and tigers. "Sounds fascinating. What makes you want to give it up for teaching?"

"All the cute baby pictures I've been seeing," he said, staight-faced. "Even my junior colleagues seem to have 'em. Kids, wives, bungalows with barbecues on the patio. It's time I found out what I've been missing." His dimple appeared, unexpectedly. "Not that I'd go so far as ever wanting a mortgage."

"But you wouldn't mind the marriage part. The children—"

"If she were the right kind of woman."

"You've never met her? In all your travels?"

"I thought so. Once or twice."

She felt a stab like jealousy, which was preposterous. "What happened?" she said quickly.

He thought for a bit. "In the end the urge to conquer the horizon proved stronger than the attraction."

"She didn't want to go with you?"

He looked distant, away in some place where she couldn't follow. "It doesn't come easily to most women. Picking up and moving on."

"We're natural-born nest-builders, you mean?"

"No offense," he said.

She wasn't offended. It was certainly true in her case. For the first time the knowledge made her a little sad. As if she, and not Hunt, were the one missing something in life. All the places she'd never see, experiences she'd never have! The people she'd never meet—although right now none of them seemed important compared to the one sitting opposite her.

"The trick to moving around a lot," he was saying, "is to do it light. Enough clothes to get by. A few books . . ."

"And a sleeping bag," she finished, shaking her head. She'd been startled, seeing the olive bag laid out on top of Margaret's peach satin spread. The sheets underneath, when she checked, had not been slept in. He grinned. "Even as a boy, I never liked making my bed."

The tea arrived, and with it rice cakes, and honey in little yellow pots that had china bees on the lid. She poured for them both.

"Don't you have some kind of home base? A place to come back to. Family." The way she had the cottage, and Margaret and Rene.

"The West Coast," he said, swirling honey over his cake. "My parents keep a room for me over the garage." He smiled, more at himself than at her. "Something about the crash of the waves and those incredible sunsets that draws me back."

She nodded. She'd wondered about the leather-framed photograph on the night table, of breakers foaming up a rocky shore to a rambling white house. A squirrel emerged from under the lobelias and crouched next to Hunt's shoe, paws tucked against its furry gray middle.

"What *is* it about you?" she said.

His pupils gleamed from under lowered lids. "Maybe I give off signals."

She could vouch for that! She frowned, watching the paws accept a crumb of cake from his fingers. "As long as you're not broadcasting rental accommodations."

"I wouldn't dare." He laughed. "I bet you listened to my seashell while you were checking out the sleeping bag."

"Yes." She went pink at the admission. But why not? She'd had to pick up his things when she dusted, among them a dawn-flushed cowrie shell lying on the dresser. "Once when I was six, a neighbor brought one home from a cruise. I used to look inside, trying to catch a a glimpse of what it was I heard."

She could tell from the way his eyes crinkled that he was picturing the little girl she had been, and liking what he saw. He refilled their cups. "Tell me. Isn't the grown-up March ever tempted to see what's out there in the big wide world?"

Oh yes, she was tempted! Right now, half lost in his sunny brown gaze, she could easily have dropped everything and gone away with him to some of those places he'd mentioned. She swept her lashes down, like blinds to shut him out. "Out of the question! I've got a business to run. Responsibilities to my customers and staff."

His fingers touched the back of her hand, making a tiny flame leap in her veins. "What about your responsibility to March Briarwood? It's a poor life, if we never take time to stand and stare. There's a poem about that, too."

"Davies. We had him in school. Everyone does." She drew her hand out of danger and looked pointedly at her watch. "Speaking of time—I really ought to be going."

He sighed and glanced over his shoulder for the waiter. "Of all the women I've met, you are without a doubt the most single-minded."

"And you've met your share," she retorted, stung. He'd as much as told her so. Still, she wished she hadn't said it—as though she cared one way or another. The uncomfortable silence between them was broken by the appearance of the waiter with the bill. March moved to Hunt's side as they left the terrace.

"Please. Don't think I didn't enjoy this. The tea, the lovely surroundings. Our conversation."

"Did you?" His face softened. "Come with me— down to the river."

"Hunt—"

"Just for a few minutes."

She'd let Mrs. Golding wait this long; a little longer wouldn't matter. The whole afternoon was a dream. They followed a path through the trees where impatiens spilled out of white garden urns. Her arm tingled when it brushed against his. Water lapped at a half-sunken pier in the sun and mallards paddled in the reedy shallows. The air was heady with the tang of fallen leaves. She couldn't remember when she had last felt so glad to be alive.

"Imagine this place existing in the heart of Weatherfield!"

"Don't tell me you've never been here before? Not even with some enterprising young man?" he teased.

"No." Her smile faded. Kent liked restaurants that made their diners appear rich and successful, and nature was fine in its place, which was mostly through a car window.

"Seems to me," said Hunt, "you've been going out to the wrong places. With the wrong men."

She tossed her head. "I suppose you think you could do better!" If she'd known about the challenge sparkling in her eyes, she would have been mortified.

"I might," he said, and turned her face gently toward his. "Given a chance." His sleeves were pushed back and his muscular forearms glinted with short golden hair. She looked up, straight into his eyes.

The sensation was a like a burst of light, a revelation. She was conscious with heightened awareness, as she had been that first day in The Cedars' kitchen, of herself as a woman and of him as a man. When he bent his head to kiss her, it seemed like the most natural thing in the world for him to be doing.

His lips moved on hers with slow exploratory strokes, fueling the small fires she felt whenever he touched her. She stirred with involuntary pleasure and his arms tightened around her, bringing her close. The hard wall of his chest was a shock, the thudding beat of his heart another. He slid a hand down her spine and she relished the warm, sweet sensation. His lips were coaxing now and promising, and she was kissing him back, discovering the taste and texture of his mouth and liking them very much. Her hands rose and clasped themselves about his neck.

Oh, Hunter, she thought. *Oh, Hunt.*

A long time later, or maybe it was minutes only, they broke off the kiss.

She gave him a shaky smile. "That wasn't supposed to happen."

"I don't know," he said. His breathing, she noticed, was as uneven as her own. "I thought it was pretty inevitable myself. Something on the order of birds flying south in fall. Or roses blooming in June."

She couldn't think of an argument to refute that and

she didn't try. Hand in hand, they walked back to the Range Rover.

Anna Rose's hatchback was still in the driveway, even though it was after five. March gave her face an apprehensive glance in the rearview mirror, as if Hunt's kiss might show in some way. She needn't have worried. Anna Rose had other developments on her mind.

"March! Thank heaven!" She started up from the desk where she'd been contemplating the telephone with a harried air. "Where were you? I've been checking all over."

"I've just come from Warbler Woods. Mrs. Golding wasn't in."

"Just now? She called at four to say she couldn't wait anymore; she had a cocktail party to go to. March, you were planning to leave here when I did. What happened?"

"Nothing happened," she said shortly. Nothing disastrous in the sense Anna Rose meant, at any rate. March dropped her shoulder bag and pretended an interest in the day's mail. She would have preferred to sort out the missed appointment without involving her staff supervisor, only that didn't seem to be an option. "I was out with Hunt Reynolds and we . . . I got delayed."

She received a blank stare from behind the desk. "You were . . . ?"

"At Weatherfield Mall. Shopping for dishes. Scatter rugs—"

"Don't tell me he's moving!"

"Winning the lottery might be nice, too." March would have smiled if Anna Rose hadn't looked so hopeful. "No, it's an idea I had, to preserve Margaret's china. And the carpets. He called from the mall.''

''Asking for help, you mean?''

''Yes.'' The interrogation was making her feel like a guilty schoolgirl. A novel sensation and a distinctly unpleasant one. ''You know what men are, shopping! He was all set to buy Wedgwood and Aubusson. What could I do?''

''I don't understand.'' Anna Rose frowned and started removing her apron. ''That was right after lunch? Tell me it's none of my business, but how could buying a few rugs and dishes—''

''Take so long?''

March crossed to the window. Evidently she was going to have to explain the whole thing, much as she didn't want to. ''Hunt insisted we have tea—by way of appreciation, he said. At this café he knew by the river.'' She stared at the cars crawling past on their way home from work, at the sapphire-bright sky beginning to fade over the rooftops. How could she describe what it was like? A visit to another world—or this world, made inexplicably new and beautiful.

''We talked about traveling,'' she said lamely. ''The sun was shining on the water.'' *And in his eyes.* She couldn't stop seeing them, looking down at her. Or his mouth, smiling. The way it descended on hers, with inexpressible tenderness. She turned, aware that neither of them had spoken for quite some time.

''What exactly did Mrs. Golding say? I'll go over first thing in the morning.''

''It's too late for that,'' countered Anna Rose, avoiding March's eyes. ''She's already called another agency. That new CleanRight franchise? 'Somebody more reliable that she could count on.' Her words.''

"I see."

She watched Anna Rose smooth and fold her apron before dropping it in the bin. She was like that, thought March with exasperated fondness, following her into the change room; it was part of what made her good at her job. "Listen, I know you're upset. But there'll be other chances."

"It's not that." Facing the locker, her plump figure expressed disapproval even from the back. "It's Hunter Reynolds. You're interested in him, aren't you? Ever since you went there on Sunday, I've had that feeling."

"Oh, Anna Rose—I don't know! What happened this afternoon was just one of those man-woman things. It doesn't mean anything. We're not about to plunge into a . . . a relationship, if that's what you're thinking." She combed distraught fingers through her hair. Why did spelling out the facts make her feel so deprived—as though something promised had been snatched out of reach? "He isn't even my type, for heaven's sake!"

"As long as you realize that." Anna Rose's eyes filled with unexpected sympathy. "I don't care about Mrs. Golding, darn it! You're my friend, March. You've been hurt once by a man and I don't want to see it happen again."

"It won't, I promise!" Touched, March reached out and squeezed her arm.

Alone in the house afterward, she tossed the contents of the bin into the washing machine. It churned and muttered to itself in the basement, providing a counterpoint to the turmoil of her thoughts. Curled up in her father's old rocker, she watched dusk swallow the white rose on the Blanche Mallerin bush.

Hunt might not be her type, but he wasn't like Kent Harrison either. Generous and life-affirming, where Kent had been narrow-minded and insecure—he would never hurt her intentionally. Still, there were other ways for a man to hurt a woman. He was thinking of settling down, he said. What if the need to travel—and travel light—reasserted itself? She shivered and realized it was after seven and she hadn't eaten supper yet. By his own admission he'd already walked out on two relationships. Leaving broken hearts behind, she didn't doubt, remembering the warm, strong look of him in the sun. She pushed herself out of the chair, turned on some lights, and opened the fridge.

Later in bed, hands under her head and head on the pillow, she stared at the fleeing patterns of light cast on the ceiling by late-passing cars, and thought about Hunt again. His kiss. The intimate way his hand had moved over her back. How it made her feel. Full of a slow, dawning joy that promised to build and build.

Chapter Five

"You can bet your Reeboks that if Mrs. Vermeer knew, she'd be back on the next plane."

Bettina's voice, which came equipped with a built-in amplifier, carried through the hall and into the office. March stopped signing paychecks and lifted her head in alarm. Now what?

The side door slammed as Jamie followed Bettina into the change room and let his mop and bucket clatter to the floor. "I thought he was kind of cool myself. Big, trusting brown eyes. Long, silky hair. Friendly, too."

Long silky hair? Who on earth—

Bettina snorted. "You weren't the one vacuuming dog hair off the carpets."

March dropped her pen as though it were on fire and crossed the hall. This was Jamie Douglas's first Saturday at The Cedars.

"What's this about a dog at The Cedars?"

"That's what I'd like to know," announced Bettina, rummaging in her locker. She was built like a small sumo wrestler with a temperament to match. "Shedding hair like a sheep in a shearing contest. Nobody told *me* there was going to be a dog. Chipmunks, they said."

"Nobody knew, believe me!" declared March.

"What kind of dog? Big? Little? Was he there with visitors?"

"Didn't see any visitors. Just the dog, and he sure looked at home to me. Size of a pony, only hairier. Wait till it rains and those big paws track mud over the carpets!"

March groaned. "Professor Reynolds wasn't around?"

"Nope. Only those two boarders of his. Blasting the socks off us with rock music."

Jamie, who'd been returning supplies to the supply room shelves, said it was heavy metal, not rock, and he enjoyed working to music himself. In fact he was thinking of bringing his boom box next week.

"Just you try, mister," grumbled Bettina, but she was grinning as she said it. March threw up her hands and went back to the office. Frowning at the clock, she dialed. Hunt had to be home from class by now. While one part of her mind registered satisfaction that Bettina and Jamie appeared to be working out as a team, the other rehearsed questions framed with diminishing degrees of tact. Was Hunt out of his mind, allowing a dog at The Cedars?

"If that's the professor you're talking to—" Bettina stuck her close-cropped black head in the door. "—ask him what he wants done with that china stacked up in the kitchen."

"China? Oh, hello—Hunt?" She sank weakly onto her chair. "March. I understand you have a—"

"March? Hang on! I can't hear." He'd been laughing and breathing hard; the sound tickled her ear, an exciting sensation she didn't need at the moment. She shut her eyes and heard shouts and barking, followed by a crash.

"Tennis-ball hockey," he explained, back on the line.

"In the house?" she shrieked.

"What do you take me for? In the atrium."

As if trampled gloxinias and shattered skylights didn't count. "With the dog, I suppose! Which is why I'm calling," she exclaimed, and he chuckled.

"You heard about our new addition to the family, did you? Kim was under the impression your staff wasn't too thrilled."

"It's not my staff you should be worried about! Hunt, you must be aware that Rene and Margaret would never allow a dog at The Cedars."

"Rene and Margaret aren't living here right now. I am." Polite enough words, but she detected something chill and immovable about them—like the freezer she had tried once to shift while cleaning. "Surely March-maids can deal with a few dog hairs," he was saying. "Or have they got a thing about canines as well as rodents?"

"That's not the issue . . ." Impatiently, she tried a different tack. "Whose dog is it? Where did he come from?"

"Do you honestly care? I found him trying to make a living off the neighborhood garbage cans."

"He's a stray?" March's voice climbed. That could mean a whole other set of problems besides dirt and breakage: fleas, unwanted puppies—"It *is* a he?" she pressed.

"Now that, I'm sure of," he replied, and laughed while she felt foolish. "If it makes you feel any better, I've put an ad in the *Weatherfield Free Press*. Come over and check him out for yourself, why don't you?"

he added genially. "You might be pleasantly surprised."

"I don't think so."

"Come tomorrow. It's Sunday, remember? After
you've met the dog, we could go for a picnic. I know
a few other great places besides the Riverview Café."

She gave a silent groan. All those feelings she'd
been working overtime to suppress were flooding
back, double strength. "This is a business call. Have
the courtesy to keep our social lives out of it."

"Cold feet?"

She flushed. "You misled me. You told me the dog
kibble in the Range Rover was for the chipmunks."

"It was. I swear!"

"And four days later you happen to have acquired
a dog? Oh, please . . ."   ·

"Life works that way sometimes. But it's the truth.
Why would I hide a dog from you on Tuesday, and
not on Saturday?" He had her there. Cornered, she
switched to the offensive. "Another thing. What's that
china Bettina says is standing around the kitchen?"

"The stuff we bought at the mall. The seagulls.
You're not going to tell me you've forgotten? Our first
set of dishes?" His tone took on an intimate quality.
"The duvet you rejected?"

"I remember." Only too well! She cut him short.
"You mean you haven't put them away yet?"

He sighed, a man wronged. "Put away where? Have
you looked in your sister's cupboards? I'd be lucky to
squeeze an eggcup in there."

"You could take out the Royal Copenhagen. I don't
imagine you're planning to serve a formal dinner any
time soon. Store it in boxes till the Vermeers get
back."

"Boxes?" He sounded doubtful.

"Use the ones the new dishes came in."

"Won't things rattle around and break?"

"Not if you use paper." March rubbed her fingers over her forehead in an effort to forestall a headache. Was he being purposely obtuse? On the other hand, what would Hunt know about storing china, when he'd never so much as owned a coffee mug? It could be a disaster. Why was it that every phone call to The Cedars led to a chain of complications?

"Maybe you could stop by and show me what to do. Get me started," he suggested. "Removing the good stuff from the cupboards would sure cut down on the temptation to use it," he added innocently when she didn't respond. "Say tomorrow at two?"

She didn't actually hear herself agree, but he said, "Great! See you then," just as though she had, and hung up.

Apparently she was once again committed to spending an afternoon with Hunt Reynolds. In spite of her best efforts. The man was a sorcerer, she decided, going into the kitchen to make up her weekly grocery list. A caster of spells, an enchanter. Dreamily she stared at the potatoes in the bin, seeing instead his warm enquiring eyes, the dimple in his chin. She had the strangest sensation in her head. As if a beautiful wordless melody had begun to play.

"Schubert's 'Song Without Words'," announced Hunt, greeting her at the front door. He waved to indicate the graceful piano chords wafting from the speakers. "Frank was a contemporary of Ludwig's. Like it?"

"Oh. Lovely," she said. It couldn't be, but for one

startled instant she'd thought it was the same tune she'd heard in her head yesterday. "Want to give me a hand with this?"

"Paper. Marchmaids thinks of everything!" He scooped the bundle out of her arms so she could take off her jacket.

"I got it from a customer who moved last week."

He was looking very spruce. A moss-colored shirt in a soft knit material outlined his big sloping shoulders, and his thick gold hair was neatly combed back. She had the feeling that he, too, had prepared carefully for this encounter. Ten minutes at least she'd spent in front of the cheval glass, trying on and discarding various combinations, before settling on slim navy corduroys teamed with a crisp white shirt and an embroidered vest. She glanced around the atrium for signs of destruction.

"So where is your new lodger? Aren't dogs supposed to check who you let in the door?"

"Kim and Chen took him to the park. One shock at a time, I figured. The kitchen first. Ready?"

"Good heavens," she murmured. Eight place settings really added up. Plates and bowls and cups perched wherever he had unpacked them, giving the impression that a flock of seagulls had landed. Nesting in excelsior on the turkey platter was the gravy boat he'd insisted on buying.

"You see, the problem—" He flung open the cupboard doors to reveal fully occupied shelves. "What is it about kitchens? Some kind of law in force—like nature abhors a vacuum?"

March laughed. "The same law that operates inside women's clothes closets. You take that end and I'll take this."

Clearing a space on the counter, she showed him how to wrap a few pieces at a time. "Hey, this is fun," he said, getting the hang of it. Smothering a teapot in a paper cocoon, he wiggled Groucho Marx eyebrows at her. "A man could get used to being part of a team around the house."

Exactly what she had been thinking, only about herself. "Don't forget the lid," she said, holding it out topped with its trademark mushroom. Their fingers touched and electric sparks raced up her arm. All this togetherness was getting out of hand. "Why don't you put the new dishes on the shelves, while I finish up with these," she said, desperate to create some distance between them.

Amusement spiked his glance. "I can see why you're a CEO, Ms. Briarwood."

What was he saying? That she was too bossy? Her glance fell on a seagull drowning in water next to the fridge. "Doesn't that dog have a dish of his own?" she snapped.

"He didn't come with one. Only the coat on his back." Hunt looked at her quizzically. "You don't care much for dogs, do you?"

"I've never owned one. But I see what they're capable of doing to people's homes."

"Nothing worse than what people do," he remarked, and he was right about that. She scribbled ROYAL COPENHAGEN on the last of the boxes.

"Wouldn't the animal shelter have taken him in?"

He straightened up. "Have you any idea how long they keep unclaimed animals in there?"

She shook her head and he said, "Forty-eight hours. After that it's game over. Dog-and-cat heaven in the sky."

"I—I didn't realize."

"Sorry. I tend to be big on Life with a capital L. For everybody and everything." As if she hadn't noticed! "If you're done with the crown jewels," he said, taking the box from her, "why don't I give you a tour of The Cedars' new user-friendly living room?"

She followed him, chastened but glad, too. More people on the planet should be big on Life and she liked the idea that he was one of them. Astonishing, the difference the rugs and throws made!

The room had taken on an air of relaxed informality. Even the pop cans lurking about seemed homey, part of the decor. "It looks—what—like you now. Instead of Margaret and Rene," she told him, and he laughed.

"I'll take that as a compliment."

Unfortunately the new look extended to art objects as well. A Venetian glass tulip held peanut shells and the vase that had survived Dire Straits doubled as a bookend for Advanced Lotus I and II. Saint Francis, who'd migrated to the dining room, had acquired a tennis visor. It drooped over one eye like a rakish halo. March's fingers itched to undo the indignities.

"Wouldn't it make sense to take some of the more fragile things out of circulation? We've got some empty cartons left."

"Listen. Just because I'm a wildlife biologist doesn't mean I'm a total philistine. I happen to enjoy having a bit of art around."

"At the rate it's doing double duty, that may not be much longer." She plucked the visor from Francis's head and handed it to him. "Wasn't that hippo propping open the door to the den one of Rene's African collection?"

He groaned. "Maybe you've got a point. I had some first-year students in for a study session last night."

Thank heaven, she thought, lightheaded with tiredness and relief as Hunt carted the last box away for safekeeping. At least Margaret and Rene would still have treasures to come home to. She went into the kitchen to sweep up excelsior and was startled to discover the clock said twenty past five.

"I don't know about you, but I could eat one of those hippos," announced Hunt, reappearing. "Do we dine in, or out?"

She smothered an urge to say "either sounds wonderful" and reached for her jacket. "We've been through all this. I am not going out with you."

He studied the expression on her face and grinned. "That means in. Excellent choice—I've been looking for a chance to show off my fritata."

"I'm serious, Hunt. Let me pass!"

"So am I." He blocked the door, arms spread playfully wide as she attempted to dodge around him. "There's nothing frivolous about fritata. I'm told Spanish working people eat it all the time."

Laughter burst from her; she couldn't help herself. Of all the ridiculous arguments for them to be having! Both of them tired and grubby, both of them ravenous and going off to eat alone after having spent an afternoon practically in each other's pockets.

"You win," she said, and tossed her jacket on the chair. She headed for the powder room, leaving Hunt triumphantly pulling out the frying pan. By the time she returned, hands and face washed, hair restored to a glossy sheen and Scarlet Ribbons lipstick freshly applied, the kitchen was fragrant with the aroma of frying onions and he was chopping red and green peppers. She eyed the tea towel wrapped snugly around his lean, mobile hips and she felt a tremor of deep emotion at the cozy, domestic scene.

"What can I do? Set the table?"

"Nope. Already taken care of." He pressed a glass of Spanish sherry into her hand, his face alive with pleasure and exertion. "Tonight we eat in The Cedars Bodega."

Mystified, she decided to wait and see.

Perched on a stool, sipping the sweet fiery liquid, she watched him add beaten eggs to the sautéed vegetables and pour the mixture into a baking dish. Kent had said once he didn't know what the big deal was about cooking—he knew how to operate a coffeemaker and put a frozen dinner in the microwave as well as any woman. But that wasn't on a level with what she was witnessing here. In rapid order, Hunt constructed a salad, piled plates onto a tray, and just as a bell signaled the fritata was done, drew a cork from a bottle with an exuberant pop.

"Por favor, señorita," he said, handing her the bottle, and they wound their way into the solarium, a festive procession of two.

March flashed him a look when she saw the candles blooming in a bowl of sand and the table set with red linen napkins and Margaret's sterling silver.

"You had all this dreamed up and ready before I even got here today," she accused, as he pulled out her chair with a Latin flourish.

"Naturally." He whisked the napkins out of their long-stemmed glasses and poured the wine. "You can't fault a man for being prepared. It's drummed into us as Boy Scouts."

Music spilled into the room as he pressed a switch.

She tested the fritata and sighed. "It's not easy, being annoyed with somebody who can make eggs taste like this."

"Why try?" His pupils danced disarmingly in the soft pool of light and she hurried to change the subject. "That's not one of Ludwig's pieces you're playing."

"In a bodega? Heck, no! That's Mañuel de Falla. *Nights in the Gardens of Spain.*"

He'd planned every detail as carefully as though he were laying a siege, she thought, detecting basil on the tomatoes. Worse still, the siege was taking effect. She could feel herself mellowing as guitars added their voice to the orchestra's, and there didn't seem to be a thing she could do about it. Like moonlight on the bougainvillea leaves and a warm breeze blowing over her skin, it felt.

"You may be right. What you said the other day. About life being more than work," she said. "Look at you. Animals, music, cooking, travel—is there anything you don't enjoy?"

He laughed. "I guess you'd have to meet my parents to know why. Dad's a hospital administrator whose idea of relaxing after a day's work is to play a little pickup Mozart on the violin with his friends. Mom's into worthwhile causes, and on the side she collects strays. Human *and* four-footed. Growing up, I recall the house was always full of homeless cats and musicians between jobs."

"Your father didn't object?"

Hunt shrugged. "Every so often he'd put his foot down and Mom would tactfully send everybody on their way. Not before she'd done her best to pair them off." His face looked fond as he reflected. "Mom thinks going through life alone is just about the worst fate that can befall a living creature. I remember once—'' He launched into an anecdote about her efforts to match an elderly lady flutist with a genteel bit of Persian fluff, only to have her go off with a one-eared bull terrier. March laughed till the tears started.

''Your mother sounds like a dear. You realize you're one of her failures?''

''She lives in hope.'' Hunt's gaze across the candle flame was tender and she held her breath for what he might be about to say, but it was only a question.

''And your childhood, March? What was it like?''

''A lot less exciting than yours. More conventional. My father managed a neighborhood hardware store, and there was never a great deal of money. Lots of love, though, and we had our share of laughter. Until our parents died, anyway.''

He poured the last of the wine into their glasses. ''Care to talk about it?'' he said simply.

She did, she realized. Because Hunt was the one doing the asking.

''Margaret and I were nineteen and fifteen when it happened. Mom and Dad were flying to Florida. They'd never been on vacation, just the two of them together. The morning they left, there was a snowstorm—one of those March blizzards? Five minutes after takeoff, their plane crashed.''

''I'm sorry.'' His eyes were full of compassion. ''You had no other family?''

''No one close.''

Shock and grief weren't all they'd had to deal with. Her father's insurance had barely covered the funeral expenses; his bank account hadn't held much more. Over the years he'd sunk all his money into the cottage.

She looked at Hunt; it seemed important to make him understand. "Margaret dropped out of Arts at college and got a job at the gallery. That's where she met Rene. We could have sold the house, I suppose . . ." She raised slender shoulders in the white shirt and let them fall. "But Emery Street was home—a last link with family. As soon as I finished school, I went to work at the one thing I knew. Housecleaning. At first it was just a way to earn a living. But then I got the idea of turning it into a business. I liked the independence, the challenge."

"And you never looked back," he commented softly.

"No." She drained her glass. She didn't want his admiration and certainly not his sympathy. It was beginning to dawn on her that what she wanted from him was a lot more dangerous to her peace of mind. Taking refuge in the music, she said, "In all your travels, have you ever been to Spain?"

"Not yet. But I'm thinking about it. They've got this superb wildlife preserve in the north."

That was not the answer she wanted to hear. She pushed her plate away and, registering her change of mood with a faint lift of his brow, Hunt said, "Coffee?"

While he was in the kitchen, she wandered about the room. Night in the gardens of Spain must be like this, she decided. Exotic foliage forming mysterious dark groves, and the blossoms on the orange tree breathing out a subtle perfume. The chipmunks were awake, rustling in their cage. Two of them sat on the hollow log, nuzzling each other affectionately. She was aware of Hunt returning and her nerves tingled with the sense of his nearness.

"Everybody needs somebody," he said quietly. "Not only chipmunks. You've been on your own a long time. Hasn't there been anybody in your life? Some special man to take you in his arms at the end of the day?"

"At first I didn't want anyone. I was too busy. Too tired, some days. Then, well—there was a man. But it didn't work out."

"A customer. The one responsible for the no-dating policy," he guessed shrewdly.

He'd put a new CD on the player and different guitars now were playing "Spanish Eyes," a favorite of hers although he couldn't know that. When his hands closed around her waist and he turned her to face him, she realized she'd been expecting it. From his expression, she thought he was going to kiss her again, and she would have liked that, in spite of her resolutions.

"Not all men are the same, you know."

"No," she whispered. Unsure suddenly, she dropped her gaze.

"But you're not convinced."

It wasn't a question and she didn't have to answer. His hands shifted on her back and they started dancing together, moving as smoothly and naturally in each other's arms as though they'd been doing it forever.

"How long has it been, since you were out with him?"

"Half a year."

It was the night of the annual Weatherfield Life service awards banquet. Kent Harrison had wanted to introduce her to the head table, but only on condition that she not tell them her occupation. "Say you run a secretarial service. They're going to think twice about promoting a man whose steady date cleans houses for a living.'' She had stared at him, the hall dissolving around her. As though after two years she were finally seeing him for the first time. ''Maybe they should. Think twice,'' she'd told him. Turning on her heel, she had marched out of the building, and out of Kent's life.

Hunt must have caught the flicker of remembered hurt in her face.

He gathered her hands in his large ones and rested them securely folded on his chest. ''Long enough,'' he said. ''Life goes on.''

''Mexicali Rose'' followed ''Spanish Eyes'' as they danced in and out of the swaying shadows, their bodies touching, parting, and touching again as a slow fire kindled in her veins. After a while, still dancing, he bent his head and this time she didn't turn away. The kiss was sweet and questing in a way that satisfied and made her burn for more. His hands moved down to her hips, pulling her close. Joy clamored and swelled inside her heart.

Then the clamor was outside. Voices, barking—doors banged open and Kim and Chen and the dog burst in together.

March drew back, not sure where to look. Hunt, his voice unaccustomedly gruff, said ''Hi, Kim. Chen. Have fun?''

''Hello, Ms. Briarwood. Super!'' They filled him in on their afternoon while the dog, a golden retriever cross with a coat the color of Hunt's hair, strolled up and thrust a friendly cold nose in her hand.

''March, meet Noble. Noble, March,'' said Hunt by way of introduction as she patted the silky head.

''Noble?'' she echoed.

''From Shakespeare. 'Hark, hark the noble dog,' ''

he prompted, laughing, as though of course she knew—didn't everybody? "Shall we have that coffee now, while the boys get their supper?"

She hesitated. "If it's all the same to you, it's been a long day and I think I ought to be getting home."

Gratifyingly, his eyes told her it was not all the same to him—he was disappointed. "You don't have to run, just because Kim and Chen are back."

"It isn't that."

But it was, indirectly. Hearing the can opener whir in the kitchen, the murmur of youthful voices, she realized the spell was broken. Reality had intruded, and a good thing, too. She felt shaken to the core, thinking what their kiss might have led to if Kim and Chen hadn't come in when they did. "Staff meeting early in the morning," she said, half in apology.

"Busy week ahead?" he wanted to know, helping her into her jacket.

"Thanksgiving holiday next weekend. Which means rescheduling customers." She reached for her bag, avoiding his gaze, because if she didn't, she might still weaken and stay. "Thanks for the supper, Hunt. It was very nice."

Nice. The lame little word, so inadequate to describe what had passed between them, hung in the air as he walked her out to the car, Noble trundling beside them.

"But you're still busy, regardless. Evenings, too." It was a statement more than a question.

"I—I'm afraid so."

Light from the house picked out the gold in his hair as he leaned down to her open car window. His big square hand lay on the frame, inches away. She steeled herself, her senses still raw and singing from his touch.

"Too bad about the Marchmaids policy," he said. "With the long weekend coming up. A perfect time of year to get away for a couple of days. We could follow the yellow brick road and see the fall colors. Get to know each other a little better."

"Hunt—"

She swallowed hard, her hand on the ignition key. "I won't promise anything. But I'll do some thinking and let you know."

He nodded. "I'll wait," he said. "Only don't make me wait too long."

Chapter Six

Ｈow long was too long?

March watched a brilliant orange leaf eddy down to the lawn. Three days had passed since Hunt put forward his tantalizing proposal of a shared weekend, and she still hadn't come to a decision. Not one that both her heart and her head could live with. As Thanksgiving drew closer, she was finding it hard to concentrate on her other problems.

The new CleanRight franchise, for example.

She dropped her car keys into her bag and started up her front steps. The franchise had launched a major campaign in her neighborhood and she was running into their aggressive neon-colored flyers everywhere. In stores, on parking lot fences, even at the bank where she'd just made her weekly deposit.

Another one greeted her from the hall floor. Posted through the mail slot—the nerve! With the Marchmaids logo in plain sight next to the door. She waved it at Anna Rose in the office.

" 'Low introductory rates,' " she quoted. " 'Let us show you what expert methods and up-to-date equipment can do.' " Indignantly she folded the offending paper and sent it sailing into the wastebasket. "Implying we aren't experts! Or up-to-date."

Anna Rose raised a gloomy face from her time

sheets. "Did I tell you, the Clendennings are thinking of switching to CleanRight?"

March sank onto a chair. That made the third customer this week. It was becoming an epidemic. "I'll set up an appointment with Mrs. C. See if I can't talk her out of it. Isn't it time you went home?"

"Just leaving."

Anna Rose checked the room for empty coffee mugs. "One good thing about customers decamping. Holiday scheduling isn't a madhouse this year. Speaking of which—" She disappeared into the change room and came back with her gray-and-pink checked jacket. "You are coming for Thanksgiving dinner, aren't you? Mama's been asking."

Spending holidays with the Morellos when Rene and Margaret were out of town was practically a tradition. She hadn't liked to even hint that this year might be different, for fear of hurting the family's feelings.

"I've been thinking," she said. "Maybe it's time I started building a life of my own. One that includes the holidays."

"If you're talking about eating turkey on your lonesome—forget it! Mama would never allow it." The gray eyes narrowed. "This wouldn't have anything to do with Hunt Reynolds, would it?"

"As a matter of fact—" March drew a breath and took the plunge. She owed it to Anna Rose, of all people, to be honest with her. "Hunt suggested the two of us go away somewhere together for the weekend."

Anna Rose was shocked. "I had no idea things had advanced that far between the two of you."

"They haven't, if you're assuming anything other

than separate rooms,'' said March uncomfortably.
''Hunt thought it would be an opportunity for us to
get to know each other better. That's all.''

''And you're actually considering the idea?'' Frank
disapproval replaced the shock. ''March, you're not
thinking straight! Have you forgotten what happened
with—''

''Hunt Reynolds is not Kent Harrison!'' she exclaimed. ''Do me a favor and stop comparing the two
every chance you get!'' Anna Rose paled and was silent. March trailed her to the door, red-faced. She
couldn't believe that was her voice she'd heard, yelling like that at someone who only had her best interests at heart.

''I—I haven't decided yet. If I do . . . go with him
. . . naturally I'll rescind the no-dating policy for
everybody.''

''It's up to you.'' Anna Rose shrugged and got out
her car keys. ''As long as you realize what the fallout
could be if things don't work out. Seeing as your sister
and her husband are involved.''

''Thank you. I *am* capable of doing my own thinking.''

They said a chilly good night and March watched
the hatchback swing into Emery Street. Being at odds
with her best friend and employee was more unpleasant than she'd bargained for. Already it was getting
mixed up in her mind with Hunt and how it would be
if she went away with him.

Two days later was like a three-ring circus. It was
twenty to nine by the time they had the last team organized and heading for the correct address. When
March went back in the kitchen, Anna Rose was

checking the biscuit tins for something to tide her over.

"Drop me off at the Reimers, on your way to the Clendennings?" she said in the breezy impersonal tone she'd adopted since their clash. "I'm giving Andrea a hand and parking's always a pain."

"Sure. Oreos in the red tin if you're looking." She tucked an apple into her own bag. "I want to talk to you anyway."

"You do?" Anna Rose, very fetching in a tam-o'-shanter that matched her jacket, gave her a sharp look.

March waited until they were in the car before asking, "Does your mother's invitation for Thanksgiving still stand?"

"You need to ask? Mama was planning to set a place for you regardless." The plump hand buckling the seat belt paused. "Does this mean you've turned down Hunt's offer?"

"Not exactly." March pulled out to pass a delivery van. A gusty cold wind that matched her mood was whipping people's hair and whirling stray bits of paper in the air. "I phoned The Cedars last evening and got Kim. He told me Hunt was at the airport picking up somebody from out of town. An old friend, he said."

"Oh." Anna Rose shifted in her seat. "Oh, dear."

"That's what I thought."

"Another woman, you mean."

"It's obvious, isn't it? Hunt got tired of waiting for me to decide and invited somebody else to spend the weekend with him."

"Did you leave a message?"

She'd thought hard, her cheeks burning at the speed with which Hunt had found a substitute for her company. "Only that I'd switch The Cedars' cleaning day to after the holiday. I didn't think Hunt wanted the team underfoot if he was entertaining guests.''

''I wondered why the change.'' Anna Rose reached for her carryall. ''Well. Here's where I get out. Good luck with Mrs. C,'' she called from the sidewalk. Her eyes were full of sympathy. ''And March—maybe it's for the best?''

Maybe it was, if Hunt found her as easy to replace as that. The thought didn't lessen the humiliation. And persuading Mrs. C was going to take a lot more than luck. March turned the corner feeling that a black cloud had settled in her head.

Mrs. Clendenning held out for a discount to match the rate offered by CleanRight. A harried-looking woman with a grown-out permanent, she was apologetic. ''I hate to do this to you, Ms. Briarwood. But the boys need new hockey equipment this fall and we've got to economize somewhere.''

March made sympathetic noises and drove downtown to tackle Dr. Benjamin's office. The dentist was an old family friend, and one of the few cleaning jobs she still sometimes did herself. No humbling surprises waiting for her here, she thought, and opened the door to a pool of water in the waiting room.

The aquarium had sprung a leak.

Hunt would give the stranded guppies a home if no one else did, she reflected grimly, dialing the building superintendent's number. She'd be lucky if she got to the supermarket before it closed.

Late that evening, after doing the accounts, she sank into bed too exhausted to do anything but sleep.

She awoke the next day with the aching sense that she had thrown away a chance at something magical. Not asking Hunt to call back had been a mistake. The friend could have been anyone. A man, or a friend of his parents passing through town. Kim hadn't specified. The fact that the wind had blown the clouds away and turned the weather glorious didn't help. She left the door ajar when she went out to rake the yard, on the off chance that Hunt might phone.

But he didn't. Too late, anyway, for the holiday— she couldn't let the Morellos down twice. Frowning, she leaned on the rake handle. Of course it was another woman. Lodged in her brain, the certainty was as difficult to remove as a splinter. And as painful. That night she slept badly.

"Come around noon," Anna Rose had suggested.

March decided to walk; the day seemed made for it. The Morello house was ten minutes from Emery Street, a two-story gabled Victorian brick with a wraparound porch. Tony Tremonti flung open the door.

"March, come in! The family's all here."

She smiled and followed him into the chintz-and-chrysanthemum living room. She liked Tony, with his curly dark hair and easy grin. Anna Rose's two sisters, fashionable in suede and high-necked sweaters, greeted her with hugs and drew her to meet the newest members of the clan, two babies born within days of each other last May.

"They're adorable," declared March, startled by the strength of emotion their tiny dimpled hands and the peach-down fuzz on their heads evoked in her. The older children vied for attention.

"You've grown since last Christmas," she said, straightening up to inspect them. "Maybe you're too big for Snakes and Ladders?"

"No! Never!" they chorused, and she handed them

the brightly wrapped package she'd been holding behind her back.

"That should keep them out of trouble till dinner," said Anna Rose. "Come in the kitchen. Mama wants your opinion on the gravy."

The gravy was delicious, as always, and certainly didn't need her to say so. It was Mrs. Morello's way of making her feel like family. She helped carry bowls of sweet potatoes and cranberry sauce into the dining room, along with more Italian dishes like eggplant parmigiana. When everyone was seated, Mrs. Morello herself, flushed and beaming with her apron off and her rings on, brought in the turkey. The seagull platter swam into March's mind, and with it, visions of Hunt wielding the carving knife in Mr. Morello's place.

Laughing over the wineglasses, as she'd seen him do, and toasting his friend—

"March, you're not eating!" Lucia Morello had the same measuring gray eyes as her daughter. "You don't care for the eggplant—"

"Leave our guest be, Mama," interrupted Tony kindly. "She's had enough stress from that new CleanRight bunch."

March threw him a grateful glance, but Mrs. Morello wasn't put off. "You work too hard at that job! Every day I tell Anna Rose. When are you going to take some time off and find a nice man? Have some nice babies?"

"Mama!" chided her daughters.

When indeed! March laughed shakily and said if she found a man as nice as the Morello sons-in-law, she'd think about it. After the pumpkin pie, tiramisu, and coffee, the young people wouldn't let her help with the cleaning up. Proudly they showed her the dishwasher they'd chipped in to buy their mama for her birthday. In the living room, the babies were wide awake and the older children took turns giving them their bottles. As soon as she decently could, March thanked her hosts and made her farewells.

Anna Rose saw her to the door.

"You're leaving early because of Hunt, aren't you? I can see it in your face. Darn man makes you unhappy even when he's not around."

"Especially then," murmured March, leaving her friend frowning after her.

She walked home through autumn leaves drifting down on the quiet holiday streets. She'd been naive to suppose the Morello family could take her mind off Hunt Reynolds. They only made her more acutely aware of everything that was missing from her life. As she turned into her driveway, a red-and-white vehicle slowed beside her.

"Hi, pretty lady," said the driver, leaning his head out.

"Hunt!" she exclaimed. She tried to conceal her delight and failed.

He parked the Range Rover and got out, too large and solid in blue jeans and an Aran sweater to be a figment of her imagination. "Tried to get you on the phone," he said. "When you didn't answer I figured you might be outside, raking."

"I thought you were busy. Kim said—"

"He neglected to tell me till dinner today that you'd called. March, why the devil didn't you call again?" He looked at her, his warm brown eyes lingering over the details as though he, too, needed to reassure himself. "I said I'd wait and I did. Right until this morning."

She felt suddenly shy. "But Hunt, what about your friend? The one—"

"Kim told you about Sid?" He laughed. "Oh, Sid and I go back a long way together. Too long for me to have to play the entertaining host."

Sid for Sidney. So much for the torments of jealousy she'd put herself through! The clouds on her horizon were rapidly thinning.

"Dinner, you said. Did you cook a turkey? Did you use your platter?" Relief was making her babble, but she didn't care.

"Sid thought it might be fun to go out instead. To the Weatherfield Arms." He made a comical face. "You're familiar with the hotel? Wraparound mahogany and crystal chandeliers. Waiters in black and a pianist in the lounge playing 'Harvest Moon.' "

She smiled. Definitely not his scene.

"And you?" he wanted to know. His gaze traveled from the cropped jacket and wide skirt of her hunter-green corduroy suit down to her sleek stockinged legs and narrow black pumps. "I take it you found somebody to spend Thanksgiving with?"

He sounded less than thrilled by the idea, and her eyes danced. "I did. A whole family of somebodies. Tony and Anna Rose and her parents. Her sisters and their husbands plus two babies and four older children," she informed him, and he threw back his head, laughing.

His arm pulled her close and she didn't draw back. "A day with me would have been a lot more restful," he said, over the top of her head.

Restful was not the word she would have used. Already his hand on her rib cage was causing the most extraordinary commotion.

"But never mind, you're with me now," he murmured, losing half the words in her hair.

"I'm glad," she said in a small voice, hiding her face against his shoulder. The rough-soft texture of his sweater was a revelation, and so was the clean outdoor male scent of him.

"Any particular reason?" he enquired, and tipped up her chin to look in her eyes.

"I missed you," she answered simply.

It felt like the most daring thing she had ever said to anyone, and the response didn't surprise her. Cupping her face in his hands, he kissed her. But the kiss itself was a surprise—she had no idea a man could kiss with such simultaneous tenderness and authority—and so was the eagerness with which she kissed him back.

"Hunt," she stammered, pulling away at last. "The neighbors . . ."

"You're right." He grinned, unabashed. "Let them celebrate their own Thanksgiving. This one is ours." He pushed himself away from the fender on which he'd been leaning and swung open the passenger door. "Hop in," he ordered.

"Now? Like this?" She glanced down at herself. No bag, nothing but a comb and a tissue in her pocket, along with her house key.

"Why not? I'll look after you," he said, pulling the seat belt out for her. He would too, she thought. She hadn't felt that about a man since her father died. His big square-tipped hands were light on the steering wheel as he backed into Emery Street. He handled the Range Rover the way he handled everything else—chipmunks, cooking, kissing—with an easy confidence.

"Do I know where we're going?" she asked, as they headed for the suburbs.

"We're following the yellow brick road." He smiled at her sidelong and switched on the CD player. "What else?"

She leaned back and gave herself up to happiness. Ages had passed since she'd been for a drive in the country and she couldn't recall it ever having looked so radiant. Apples glinted crimson under the blue bowl of the sky and the fields were stubbled with gold. Hunt had the windows open and a rushing wind mixed with the rollicking duet of flute and drums. Impossible to talk! But every time their glances met, a spark of communication more intimate than words passed between them.

Lake Huron glittered through a row of poplars. At Summer Bay, they slowed and turned off onto a side road. Cottages with names like Snug Harbor and Dream Awhile topped a bluff overlooking the water. The village itself lay at the foot of a winding hill. Hunt parked in the deserted lot of a boating supplies store.

"Feel like walking?" he said.

Her hand slipped naturally into his as they wandered the main street. Art and craft shops with mullioned windows sheltered under the trees. At the corner, the red brick Summer Bay Inn offered special rates for honeymooners.

"I'll bet they've got some takers," drawled Hunt, and something lazy and inviting in his tone made her heart beat faster.

But it was late in the year for honeymooners, and almost the only people they saw were at the marina, readying their boats for winter storage. "That's what I miss the most. The water," remarked Hunt.

Resting his elbows on an upturned hull, he watched the long jade swells heaving endlessly toward shore. He looked like a man thinking about going on a thousand-mile journey. March shivered as a cloud drifted over the sun.

"Cup of coffee?" he suggested, returning from wherever he'd been.

The beachside restaurant was closed till May, a sign said, but around the corner they found a hole-in-the-wall snack bar selling ice cream. "Chocolate," she decided, and he bought two double-dip cones.

Throwing an arm around her shoulder, he steered her onto the beach. Tucked in close to his side, with the sun warm again on her back and the ice cream tingling on her tongue, she felt bold enough to ask the question that was never far from her mind these days.

"Do you know yet, where you'll go after Weatherfield?"

"I'm working on it," he said.

Next to an enormous boulder he ducked his head and kissed her. "Mmm. Chocolate," he said gruffly, and she saw the desire in his eyes.

He flicked the last of his cone into a trash can, and bracing himself against the rock, he pulled her roughly into his arms at such an angle that she was obliged to lean on him. He was all hard planes and taut muscles and she was all yielding softness, and when they kissed a second time, it was electrifying.

Breathlessly, she pushed herself free.

"Tell me—tell me about growing up by the ocean," she said, conjuring up the leggy golden-skinned boy he must have been. All those years of his life she knew nothing about!

He smiled, willing to bide his time. "It was magic,"

he said. "Picnics on the beach. Going sailing in the little cockleshell boat my father and I built that terrified my mother. The water a different mood every time you looked. The sunsets that went on till midnight."

"Nice," she said grudgingly. But hardly unique to the West Coast. Her chin tilted. "Did you know they call Summer Bay the sunset capital of Canada?"

"Really?" he said.

They walked again, arms linked around each other's waists. Past a bend in the shore so that they were the last two people left on earth. A breeze painted racing brushstrokes of indigo on the lake. Only a faint dazzling line marked where the water ended and the sky began. Gulls soared and the bluffs climbed up from the sand, with here and there a gable or a chimney peering down at them.

"Looking out over the Pacific from my bedroom window," he teased, "on a clear day I could see all the way to Japan."

"That's nothing. On a clear day from the top of the bluffs you can see the coast of Michigan."

Amusement tugged at the corner of his mouth. "Can't get much clearer than today. Shall we put it to the test?"

She grinned. "Why not?"

She started across the beach and up the bluffs at a speed that left him scrambling to catch up. A path zigzagged between the rocks and shrubs, clawing for a foothold. Her shoes, she thought!

"Maybe," she gasped, slowing for breath, "this isn't such a good idea. What if somebody's at home up there?"

He craned to look at the railed deck coming into view. "Not likely. That's a lighthouse."

"A lighthouse!"

She hadn't known there were any left on the lake. They clambered over the rise and there it stood, a white tower topped by an octagonal glass dome. Abandoned, apparently. The windows of the adjoining frame house shone blank. March waded through goldenrod to peer inside.

"The kitchen, I think. It's got one of those old wood-burning ranges. And a pegged-maple floor. In pretty fair shape, considering."

Hunt sprawled on the veranda step, grinning up at her with the sun in his eyes.

"You never quit, do you?" She tried not to notice the long blue-jeaned legs and narrow male hips.

"Quit what?" she said.

"Looking at the world in terms of whether it's clean and well cared for."

"It's my job! My vocation!"

She brushed yellow pollen off her skirt. Smug, that's what he was! He'd folded his arms behind his head, utterly relaxed, and she shot him a challenging look. "I thought you came up here to see Michigan."

"So I did." The gleam was back under his lashes and it had nothing to do with Michigan.

"Then how come you're lounging down there gaping at me instead?"

He rose up with a shout of laughter and made a grab for her. But she was already off and running, around the house to the far side, her skirt swirling about her knees. He was faster, but she was agile, dodging through the long grass. Under a row of poplar trees, he caught her. Flung an arm about her waist and pulled her down with him, shrieking and laughing in a tangle of limbs.

"March, oh March," he said hoarsely.

He covered her face with kisses—her forehead, her eyelids, her chin. Still laughing, she struggled by turns to extricate herself and kiss him back. Until she was kissing him only, with an explosive abandon that matched his own.

"You're beautiful. Like the empress of poppies." He mouthed the words against her lips, as though he couldn't bear to break off contact between them.

If she was, she thought, it was because he made her so. She'd never felt like this before.

"March?"

He gazed down at her, eyes heavy-lidded. "I don't want this day to end. You know that, don't you? Stay with me."

Something stilled inside her. Overhead the leaves trembled and shimmered, like brass coins suspended in the windy blue.

"Now?" she said. "Here?"

"Actually, I was thinking of the Inn. Romantic though it might be out here. I was hoping we could stay the night, salvage some of that weekend together I'd talked about."

"At honeymoon rates," she said shakily.

He nodded. He didn't laugh, and she liked him for that. "We could watch the sunset over dinner. Take separate rooms, hard as that'll be for me. And drive back to Weatherfield first thing in the morning before anybody even noticed we were missing."

Her heart dipped and righted itself. Was that what she wanted? She struggled to a sitting position, feeling suddenly vulnerable. The shadows were lengthening on the sun-warmed wall opposite.

"I heard a song like that once. About a small hotel,'' she said cautiously. She hummed a few bars off-key—she'd never been good at music.

''Not one of Ludwig's. But nice.'' His expression was tender as he watched her face. ''Will you, March? Stay with me?''

The problem was, she wanted to be with him always, and not simply for one romantic outing. And how could she, when he was a man who moved around the country—the world, it seemed—as easily as rolling up a sleeping bag?

''Your friend would notice,'' she hedged. ''Won't he be expecting you back this evening?''

Hunt stood up. Pulled her to her feet. Plucked a wisp of dried grass out of her hair. ''She. Sid is a woman. Didn't Kim tell you?''

''A woman?''

''Sidonie Bell. But don't worry about it. I told her I might be late.''

Sid for Sidonie. Why hadn't she thought of that? Because she hadn't wanted to. The frozen sensation inside her head made speech difficult. ''No, Kim didn't say.'' What did he mean, don't worry about it? She turned away, horribly aware that she'd come close to making the mistake of her life.

''The two of you go back a long way, you said.''

Hunt raked a hand through his hair. He seemed bemused by the speed with which the course of events had changed directions. ''We grew up together. The Reynolds and the Bells were next-door neighbors.''

''Is that why she's here? For old times' sake?''

''She needed to talk. I'm a good listener. March, forget Sid! She's not the issue right now—*we* are! This is our weekend, remember?''

Forget Sidonie? Forget a bomb had just been

dropped? How many more old friends who happened to be women who needed to talk did Hunt have in his past? Flushed with resentment, she watched the sun dip into Lake Huron.

"Our weekend! That's a laugh! Coming from a man who's spent most of it with another woman."

"You're behaving as though I arranged the whole thing. March, be fair! I had no idea. The first I knew about it, Sid was at the airport wanting me to pick her up." He fixed pained, angry eyes on her. "I came, didn't I, the minute Kim told me? It's not my fault you didn't leave a message."

Next he'd be saying it was hers. That she was too insecure. Maybe she was, where he was concerned. Also hurt and confused. Add jealous—that would explain the disagreeable sharp stab she felt whenever he said the word "she."

"I don't care how it happened. But I never did like leftovers, and that's how this feels. Anyway, Thanksgiving's over," she tacked on lamely. "There's work at the office. I'll need to get an early start."

"Fine. It's your decision. Watch your step," he growled as they started down the path to the beach. "Forget I even mentioned the Inn. It's not as though you didn't warn me."

"What do you mean?"

She looked at him. His face had gone from warm and eager to chill and stony. Like the water, now that the sun had sunk below the horizon. Like her heart, she thought in silent anguish.

"Not many women make it so clear." He was striding downhill fast. She had trouble keeping up. "Heck, you've even got a policy spelling it out! 'Customers and romance to be kept separate.' "

"Things can change," she said. "You might like to know—"

That was as far as she got. Her foot came down on a loose stone and she gave a cry. The stone went skipping and bounding down to the beach. Arms flailing, she would have gone with it, except that Hunt's big, firm hand grabbed her just in time.

"If you'd stop talking and watch where you were going," he said irritably, "I'd be able to get you back where you want to be a lot sooner."

Chapter Seven

The Duffields and the Olivers left messages on the answering machine over the holiday weekend saying they would no longer be requiring Marchmaids' services.

No explanations, but March could guess. They were switching to CleanRight, and too embarrassed to say so.

Lying sleepless long into the night, reliving the disastrous ending to her afternoon with Hunt, it was almost a relief to turn her mind to Marchmaids' problems. That made two more customers lost to CleanRight and if they hoped to survive they were going to have to go the franchise one better. Instead of offering cut-rate prices, how about extra services, free of charge? Closet clean-outs, window washing, silver polishing—choice of one per customer. March thumped her pillow and drew a mental blind over Hunt's face, which kept trying to intrude.

And why not a get-acquainted offer to attract new customers?

Free oven-cleaning, say—a job that everybody hated—as a sample of their skills. Would a woman travel halfway across the country to be with a man, if his skills as a listener were the only thing on her mind? March turned on her bedside lamp and hunted up paper and pen. She'd fight fire with fire. Make up a flyer and send it around the way CleanRight did. Not for nothing did her marching maid carry her mop like a musket! Of course, there was always a chance she was overreacting—

She awoke with a start. She'd dozed off and Hunt had sneaked back into her head. Teasing eyes half closed against the sun, eager hands pulling her toward him—She threw off the covers. Thrusting her arms through the comforting sleeves of her old flannel kimono, she made her way down to the kitchen. Over a pot of herbal tea she sat at the table working on her flyer, until finally it was seven and time to shower and dress.

She was seeing off the teams when Anna Rose, red-faced, burst in the door. She and Tony had picked this morning of all mornings to oversleep.

"Watched a movie last night. Forgot to set the alarm! We'd still be asleep if the garage hadn't called. Oh, March, I'm sorry—"

Ironic, thought March. She could have stayed at the Inn and still been back before Anna Rose. "It's all right. I was up early anyway. Join me in the kitchen for a coffee?"

Gratefully, Anna Rose took the mug. "Free of charge?" she yelped. She sank into a chair to study the neatly lettered sheet of paper lying on the table. "We'll lose our shirts!"

"It beats losing our business. And something else, while you're here . . ." March glanced at the clock and turned to rinse her breakfast dishes. "I'm officially rescinding the no-dating policy. Effective Thanksgiving."

She could feel Anna Rose's eyes boring into her back. "Why? What happened then?"

"Hunt and I drove to Summer Bay after I got back from your parents."

"March! Is *that* the reason you left early?"

"What do you think?" The accusation hurt. "Believe me, I had no idea. He came by the house, and a drive in the country seemed like a good idea. That's all." She turned off the tap and dried her hands. Her face glanced back at her from the glass-fronted cupboard. Pale, but a discreet touch of makeup concealed the trace of last night's tears. "That friend of his who came for the weekend? We were right, it was a woman. Someone he grew up with on the West Coast. Anna Rose, I'm in love with the big bear and I'm going to fight for him. Only I can't do it with my hands tied behind my back."

The clock ticked loudly as Anna Rose digested this.

"I hate to sound like a broken record, March. But I think you're setting yourself up for disappointment." She gestured, palms up. "Is he in love with you? Did he say so?"

He said she was beautiful and that he wanted her to stay. More or less what every man told the woman in his arms. March picked up the flyer. "I'm going to the printer's to drop this off. Not in actual words, he didn't. That's what I have to find out, isn't it?"

"Preferably before it's too late and he breaks your heart." Anna Rose sighed and followed her into the hall.

Her own romance with Tony had been a deep, smooth-flowing stream, with hardly a ripple to trouble it. She fastened her raincoat while March did the same. A steady drizzle was falling outside and the driveway was slick with puddles.

"All I can say is, Hunt Reynolds better wipe the

dog's paws before he lets him in today!'' she said, snapping open her umbrella.

Knowing Hunt, the odds weren't good, thought March. Maybe hers weren't much better, but she had to try. She looked somberly at her friend as they opened their car doors.

''I realize you don't trust Hunt, and you think I'm doing the wrong thing. All the same, call a meeting for tomorrow. We'll discuss the free offers and I'll inform the staff about the policy change.''

The meeting broke up in laughter when Andrea, her big-boned face wistful, said, ''I don't think it'll help. The only men I run into cleaning are over seventy and asleep in front of TV, or fifteen with acne and cramming for exams.''

There'd been a lot of good-natured joking over March's announcement. Bettina and Jamie were the last to leave.

''Policy or no—first guy to try anything funny with me, gets a punch on the nose,'' declared Bettina, clashing vacuum cleaner tubes with a belligerence that made March wince. ''You ready, Jamie? Or are you going to keep admiring yourself in that mirror?''

''Aye, aye, Cap'n Clean.'' Jamie pocketed his comb and flashed March a grin at the door. ''Gotta look my best. Just in case I run into the girl of my dreams.''

''Come *on*!'' yelled Bettina, hooking his knee with the carpet brush. ''It's The Cedars this morning, remember? The only thing you're going to run into is hard labor!''

March waved them off and shook her head. What had she unleashed on the unsuspecting populace of Weatherfield?

Still, she felt certain she'd chosen the right course as she left to collect her flyers at the printer's. Hunt was not going to accuse her again of putting business concerns ahead of him. They hadn't spoken since that awful drive home Monday. No doubt he was still smarting, just as she was, from words exchanged in anger. Well, the holiday weekend was behind them now, and with Sidonie Bell safely back in B.C. or wherever, they could talk things over, like reasonable adults this time.

She'd let him know she understood about Sidonie. Or—she frowned—perhaps she wouldn't mention her at all. She'd tell him the policy was history. Hunt would look at her in pleased surprise. After a while he'd take her in his arms and they'd kiss. March was back in the office optimistically expanding on this theme when Bettina and Jamie returned from The Cedars.

They were late, she noted. Bettina was in a black fury, she could tell from the window. She propelled her short, stocky body from behind the wheel and stumped, scowling, up the steps. Jamie followed, whistling.

March held the door. "How did it go?"

"Okay," responded Jamie, with a look at his partner.

Bettina snorted. "Okay if you don't mind being treated like a personal valet."

March was right behind them in the change room. "Professor Reynolds did that?"

"*He* wasn't there. More's the pity. Him I could handle."

Bettina let her equipment clatter to the tiles and eased herself onto the bench where she unlaced her air-pump Nikes. "It's this woman he's got staying with him. Thinks she's Lady Di. Lipstick stains on the towels, clothes all over the floor. She had me doing her laundry—sweaters and lacy stuff by hand, if you please, and didn't I do ironing? When she asked Jamie to run her an errand at the drugstore, I said no way. He was up to his knees in the carpets—" Bettina paused darkly for effect. "Somebody let the dog in with muddy paws yesterday."

"Did she say her name?" asked March with a hollow sinking feeling. As if she didn't know! "Did she say how long she was staying?"

Bettina stopped massaging her arches long enough to give her a look, faintly curious, faintly pitying.

"Tall skinny blond. You didn't know she'd moved in? She plays the harp." Bettina's brow beetled, remembering. "We had to wait with the vacuuming till she finished practicing. If she's still doing her princess-and-peasant act next week, count me out from cleaning at The Cedars! I'd hate to have to swear at a customer."

"No, we can't have that . . ."

March felt weak at the knees. Weak in the head is what she must have been, taking it for granted that Hunt's old friend was only staying the weekend. Jamie joined them from the supply room.

"Sidonie Bell, you're talking about?" he chimed in. "Gee, I'd run her errands anytime. With that sexy voice and hair down to here—" He made a chopping motion below his waist. "And did you get a load of her Chanel No. 10?"

Bettina slung a Nike at him in disdain. "How would a kid like you know what Chanel No. 10 smells like?"

"I'm older than I look." Jamie caught the shoe in

mid-flight and smirked. "Is this a love token you're sending me?"

"Give me that!"

Bettina bounced up to snatch it back, and March had the dizzying impression that everything was getting away from her, hurtling out of control. The team, the situation at The Cedars, and most of all, her relationship with Hunt. "Stop it! Both of you! You're behaving like children!"

She'd had no idea she was going to shout. Jamie, flushing under his freckles, straightened up. "Sorry, Ms. Briarwood."

Even Bettina looked chastened. Thrusting her feet in her shoes, she muttered it was time they were leaving if they wanted to grab a hamburger prior to the next job. March rubbed a hand over her forehead and escaped to the office, where she dipped into petty cash.

"Here, you two. Lunch is on Marchmaids today," she told them at the door. "And Bettina? I'll sort things out with Professor Reynolds."

She had her finger on the dial even before the hatchback disappeared down the driveway. While her indignation held and before other, less trustworthy emotions could intervene. Hunt himself answered, halfway through the second ring.

"March? I was about to call you." His tone was curt, defying interruption. "What gives? I come home to find the Humane Society at my door because the dog's running loose in the street. Sid is in tears. And the laundry room's full of unfinished wash."

March swallowed. "I beg your pardon. This is *my* call. I've got a couple of questions I want answered first."

"Such as?" he demanded, and she replied with the

first thing that came into her head. "Why didn't you tell me Sidonie Bell was staying on?"

"I wasn't aware I had to. What is this? Some new Marchmaids policy you've dreamed up to keep the customer in his place?"

She closed her eyes; bad start. "It's nothing of the kind. This is an old argument recycled. If you recall. My cleaners are not personal maids and I can't afford to let them be used as such."

"Are you implying that's what Sid did?"

Stubbornly she ignored the warning flags in his tone and plowed on. "Hunt, I don't want you to take this the wrong way, but have you considered she might actually be happier in a hotel? Where they have chambermaids and laundry service—"

"Are you serious? Nobody asks friends to move into a hotel! Listen, March. Sidonie Bell is a beautiful, sensitive human being who's been upset by your staff's rudeness. If you ask me, you've got a personnel problem on your hands. Do something to correct it or you're going to lose customers."

Was that a threat? Heatedly she said, "What I'm going to lose is more staff, thanks to Ms. Bell."

"How come, darn it," he erupted, "every time I extend the hospitality of my roof to some needy member of creation, there's trouble with your cleaners?"

"The Vermeers' roof, don't you mean?" March fired back, stung. "Maybe you should be asking Rene and Margaret that question! My staff is only trying to do their job. And while we're at it, in the future if you're going to let the dog on the carpets, have the courtesy to wipe his paws when it rains."

Hunt groaned. "I forgot! All right, you win. We'll discuss the charges—yours and mine." Abruptly he lowered his voice. "But not on the phone. May I come over?"

Her heart somersaulted in her chest. No, unwise idea. She did not want Hunt in her house, sprawled handsomely in a chair close enough to touch, while he argued the case of a beautiful young woman with hair down to there.

"I was about to go out," she informed him. "My working day hasn't ended, you know."

"As if you'd let me forget," he muttered, and she could have bitten her tongue. "We could meet somewhere," she said, compromising. "At the Industrial Mall, in twenty minutes? There's a doughnut shop next to the cleaning products dealer."

He grunted assent. She hung up and reached for her car keys. This was not how she had envisioned their next encounter.

Waiting to make the turn into the mall parking lot, she realized with painful clarity how much fantasy and romance she'd invested in daydreams of Hunt over the last few days. Sidonie Bell notwithstanding. When she emerged from the dealer's, hugging a two-gallon jug of floor wax she didn't need, Hunt strolled up from between parked cars.

All legs, and rugged sloping shoulders in a cognac-colored leather bomber jacket. The look in his eyes went straight through her.

"I'll carry that for you," he said, reaching out.

"I can manage," she mumbled, hoping that the sudden constriction in her chest was due to the jug and not to his proximity.

"Sure you can," he countered, and lifted the jug from her arms. "But you still have to unlock your hatch."

She scrabbled in her shoulder bag for the key, acutely conscious of him looming over her.

"Relax. We're here to negotiate. Not fire more shots."

She plunged her fists into the pockets of her belted navy raincoat while a private war between resentment and pleasure at seeing him raged in her head. A gust of wind ruffled his hair—the single bright spot in the gray surroundings of the mall—as he held the door.

"In that case," she said, "it might be best if we keep our personal lives out of this."

His expression was infuriatingly bland. "Suits me. A doughnut to go with the coffee?" he suggested, as they waited at the counter for a girl in a peaked cap to serve them.

"Coffee only. And I'll pay for mine."

"Make that two coffees and two walnut crullers, please," he told the peaked cap. "You didn't have lunch today, am I right?"

March eyed him defiantly. "What does that have to do with anything?"

"Quite a lot," he said, ignoring her proffered bill and digging into his pocket for the correct change. "A hungry woman is an irritable woman, in my experience," he observed, scooping up the crullers along with both cups. "Which table?"

She led the way to one by the window and plumped herself down. "What makes me irritable," she burst out, unable to dam the flood any longer, "is thinking how I let myself be driven around the countryside and kissed and invited to . . . to spend the night, by a man who just happened to have an old female friend move in with him."

So much for keeping the personal out of it. Hunt expelled a long, soft breath.

"I had no idea. You're really hurt, aren't you?"

Hurt was an understatement. March unbuttoned her coat and flung it back. "I feel betrayed. What do you think?"

He grimaced. "At least you had the good sense to turn the invitation down."

He made it sound amusing but she could see in his eyes that it wasn't. Not for him, any more than it was for her. Surely a good sign? "For what it's worth," she heard herself blurt out, "Marchmaids no longer has a no-dating policy."

"It's a start." He raised a wry brow. "Especially since I was planning to ask you again."

"You . . . were?"

"To a wine and cheese party I'm giving Saturday. A good way to celebrate a cease-fire, wouldn't you say?"

"A party. Oh. Yes." She found herself blushing. "I thought you meant . . . you were going to ask me to . . . well—"

"Go away somewhere together?" He shot her a devastating smile. "Not that I wouldn't like to. But a man's ego is a fragile plant. It needs time to recover." He leaned across the table. "March, you've got to believe me. The last thing I wanted to do was hurt you. Maybe if you'd let me explain about Sidonie . . ."

Unwillingly, she nodded and he said earnestly, "She's going through a rough time in her life. Her fiancé, a brilliant young Vancouver orchestra conductor, broke off their engagement last month. Sid was desperate for a place where she could get away from it all. The associations. The media publicity."

March, after the initial surge of pity, was unable to stifle the uncharitable question that sprang to her lips. "And the place she chose just happened to be with you?"

"Call it an old habit." He shrugged. "Sid was an only child. Her parents were a couple of gentle dreamers who didn't always know how to cope. Looking back, I'd say she spent as much time with our family as she did at home. Sid's a couple of years younger than I am. I suppose it's natural she came to regard me as a combination older brother and boy-next-door."

The boy next door. Raindrops slid down the windowpane, fat as tears. He was explaining about Sidonie all right, but March had the feeling he was leaving out a part about himself.

"She was in love with you, wasn't she?"

Was it her imagination, or did Hunt look evasive? "I wouldn't call it being in love, exactly. We were both still in our teens when I left for college. She might have had what's referred to as a crush. You know how it is with adolescent girls." He chased a crumb around his saucer. "Anyway, that's all in the past. Now I'm just a familiar shoulder to cry on. Poor kid. She's pretty broken up."

Not too broken up to dab Chanel No. 10 behind her ears, thought March.

"Well, that's a very moving story and I'm sorry if I jumped to the wrong conclusions. But it doesn't solve the problem of her ordering my cleaners around. Keeping them from work—"

He leaned back with an impatient look. "You never stop, do you? If it isn't Sid, it's the dog! That's either a darn touchy staff you've got, or somebody's been embroidering the facts.''

"Bettina's not touchy. She's a tough cookie. And she doesn't lie, if that's what you're insinuating. Why would she? She's only interested in doing her job. Which does not include hand-washing your guest's lingerie—''

"Fine. I'll have a word with Sid,'' he said stiffly. "But I still think you've got the story wrong.''

For two people negotiating a cease-fire, their relationship seemed dangerously loaded with live ammunition. "That's your prerogative,'' she said, pushing her cup away and reaching for her bag. "Doesn't Ms. Bell have a job or something to get back to?''

"Sid isn't into jobs.'' He appeared shocked by the suggestion. "She's a harpist taking postgraduate music theory. In fact, she's thinking of applying for a course at Weatherfield U.''

March stared at him, feeling sick. "She is?''

"That's the official reason I'm giving the party Saturday. So the dean of music and some of the people influential in local music circles can hear her play—''

"Which should guarantee her chances of being accepted. I understand. Because of course she plays divinely.'' March scraped back her chair and plunked some money on the table. "That's for my coffee. And the doughnut.''

"Cruller. Which you didn't eat.'' Hunt rose to his feet, close enough to make her head swim. "What do you mean, you understand? How do you know she plays divinely?''

"How else would she play the harp?'' She attempted a smile that didn't quite come off. "A woman

who's talented, beautiful, sensitive, and—I almost forgot—has long blond hair down to her waist.''

Hunt's eyes narrowed.

''March, what's gotten into you? I'd say you were
jealous, if I didn't know you had more sense.''

Jealous of the ease with which Sidonie Bell had
moved back into his life and was threatening—being
encouraged, even—to become a permanent fixture?
Yes, darn right she was!

''Certainly not,'' she lied. She was raising her voice
again; it was getting to be a habit around Hunt. People
in the shop were looking at them. She spoke more
quietly.

''I've said my piece, and you've said yours. Or
Sid's. Whoever's. So there's no point in further dis-
cussion, is there?'' She started for the door.

He grabbed his jacket and caught up with her outside. ''Maybe if you'd take the trouble to meet Sidonie
for yourself on Saturday. Before rushing off half-
cocked with an opinion—''

''You're sure she wants to meet me? Somebody
who got her start cleaning houses for a living?''

''March!''

Eyes swimming with traitorous tears, she plunged
off the curb straight into the path of a van backing out
of the parking slot opposite. She froze. A scream rose
in her throat, then an arm closed around her waist and
yanked her to safety.

Hunt, breathing heavily, hugged her to him. She
was too shaken to resist.

''You seem to be making a habit lately of living on
the edge.'' His voice was rough, half muffled by her
hair.

For one blessed minute she left her head where it

was, buried against his shoulder, aware of the buttery-soft texture of his jacket and the hard muscular cage of his chest inside. Fear and misery melted away. Hunt's arms represented comfort and security—more of the things that were missing from her life. Of course, it was only temporary, an illusion.

"I—I'm fine. Really." She fumbled a tissue out of her pocket and mopped her eyes and nose. "Now I suppose you'll want me to be grateful to you forever for saving my life," she muttered.

He sighed and planted a kiss on the top of her head. His heart had slowed to a solid, steady beat. "If that's an offer," he said, "I won't say no."

He seemed in no hurry to release her. The man in the van, after a white-faced look through his half-open door, had driven off. Reluctantly, she disengaged herself. Hunt took the car keys out of her hand and opened the door.

"I'd settle for your presence at the party Saturday night instead," he said.

"I'll think about it," she told him, sliding behind the wheel.

He nodded, his face grave in a way she'd never seen it. As she merged with traffic, he was still standing where she'd left him, the cognac leather jacket speckled with rain.

She was struggling to get out of her wet coat when the telephone rang. She took it in the office.

"Marchmaids. Hello?"

"March? Hunt. I had to know if you got home all right."

She sank into the swivel chair, one arm trapped in her coat sleeve. "You don't have to keep worrying about me. Just because I behave like an idiot when I'm around you."

"Now I wonder why that is?" he said softly.

Don't you know? Oh, Hunt. She shut her eyes and shook her arm free. The words "I love you" remained locked away inside her head. Since Sidonie Bell had arrived on the scene, she appeared to have lost the key. A good thing, probably. Hunt's concern didn't necessarily signify that she was anyone special to him. He was a man who cared about everybody and everything. Impoverished students, orphaned chipmunks and homeless dogs. Old flames with broken hearts . . .

"Good-bye," she said, and hung up.

Chapter Eight

"The red and black? Or the skirt and blouse?"

"If it's sophistication you're after . . ."

"Definitely. To the hilt."

"Then it's the red and black. No contest."

"That's what I thought, too."

March's new lace slip felt cool and caressing on her skin as she moved to lift the stylish cocktail dress from its hanger. Anna Rose had stayed on after work to lend moral support while she prepared for Hunt's party. She watched from the window seat as March slid her arms through the narrow, pointed black sleeves and let the shimmering raspberry folds of the brief skirt drop over her head.

"Oh, my! Straight off the cover of *Vogue.*"

"All right, do you think?" Turning to the cheval glass, March smoothed the fitted black bodice over her waist and peered critically at the long slender expanse of her legs. "Not too . . . revealing?"

Anna Rose sighed. "Not when what you've got to reveal is the right size and perfectly distributed. Even at sixteen, I never looked like that."

"If you had, Tony might not have given you a second glance. It's obvious he likes you just the way you are."

"Bless you, for that charming lie!"

Anna Rose laughed and her plump face in the glass

looked consoled. Not her mother's pearls, decided March, holding them up to her neck. Her gold locket. The one Margaret had given her the year she graduated from high school. Her final graduation. No postgraduate courses for her, unless she counted five weeks in night school to learn basic bookkeeping. She stooped to select a pair of shoes from the rack in her closet.

"March?"

"Hmm?"

Distracted, she discarded shiny strap sandals in favor of black pumps. This was a wine and cheese party after all, and not one of those glitzy cocktail affairs Kent's company was fond of holding at the Weatherfield Arms.

"No second thoughts?"

"What? About these shoes?"

"No. They're fine. About going to Hunt's party."

March sat down at her dressing table and took out eye shadow and liner. She'd been through all this in her mind a dozen times since Tuesday. "I refuse, absolutely refuse, to let myself be swayed," she told herself under her breath.

She outlined her eyes and smiled at Anna Rose's reflection. "Why should I have second thoughts? We've officially changed the policy, and as far as I know, I can sleep in late tomorrow."

"That's not what I mean and you know it! I'm the last person to begrudge you a night out. But at a party Hunt Reynolds is holding for another woman?"

"At least he was up front about it."

"Up front or up to something. Maybe he wants you there to provide damage control when the guests start throwing canapés."

"For heaven's sake! These are civilized people he's invited. Adults, not students." March sprayed Ysatis on her wrists and throat. It seemed a long time since she had worn so sophisticated a scent. "You're not telling me anything I haven't thought of myself." She stood up in a rustle of taffeta and turned to face the window. "But I'll have to take the risk. I don't want to lose Hunt by default. If running a business has taught me anything, it's to know your competition."

"I figured that's what you'd say."

Anna Rose slid off the seat and fluffed the pillows. "No earrings?" she asked, and March, reaching for her small clutch bag, shook her head. Her freshly washed hair swung in the light, glossy as jet. "None that look right."

"In that case, try these." Anna Rose handed her a small velvet box and March, eyes wide, lifted a pair of fine gold hoops from their cotton wool nest.

"I couldn't! Aren't they the ones you wore at your wedding?"

"So? Maybe they'll bring you luck. If that's what you're sure you want."

March bent to the mirror and reverently fastened them on. She gave her friend a quick hug. "If it's luck like yours, I want it."

At the door, while she was getting into her raincoat, Anna Rose said, "Promise me one thing?"

"What?"

"If somebody drops their wineglass on the carpet, you won't go for the shampoo?"

"In this dress?" exclaimed March in mock horror. Even on sale, it had cost a week's profits. "Tell you all about it Monday," she said brightly. "And don't forget to lock up."

Outside under the streetlamp, the dahlias sparkled with frost. She wondered if she wouldn't have looked better in her winter coat with its fake fur collar, instead of her drab navy. Hunt hadn't been in touch with her again. For all she knew, *he* might be the one having second thoughts about his invitation. Driving the familiar route along darkened streets, she realized her self-confidence was fading rapidly.

Misty gold light shone through the glassed-in areas of The Cedars, warming the night. The driveway was bumper to bumper with cars and she had to park half-way down the block.

Shivering with nerves and cold, she rang the bell. The muffled thump of music drowned out the chimes—in there, people were dancing and enjoying themselves. Hunt and the girl who'd once had a crush on him included. March quelled an urge to flee. Eventually the door opened and a slim young woman in a dress the exquisite color of white lilies said, "Yes?"

"I'm March Briarwood. Here for the party. Is Hunt—"

"The maid service? That March?" Blond brows arched and March felt the chill of unfriendly vibrations. "I'm afraid Professor Reynolds is busy with guests at the moment."

"Not a maid service. A cleaning agency. I own it." Her mouth felt dry. "You're Sidonie Bell, aren't you?"

"Yes." She shook back a silken skein of hair. Beautiful, Hunt had called her, and she could see why. Spring-green eyes in a face like a cool pale flower, with a cultivated voice to match saying, "If you've come to clean up you're too early."

March flushed and pushed past her, catching the

scent of Jamie's Chanel No. 10. "I don't clean up after parties. I send my staff to do that. If you'd be so kind as to hang this somewhere—" She shrugged off her coat as she spoke, mentally transforming it into a full-length mink, and held it regally in Sidonie's direction. "—I'll go and find Hunt for myself."

Her triumph was short-lived. Halfway through the atrium, it became clear that her dress was all wrong. Every other woman in sight wore slinky slacks or one of those chic skirt-and-sweater combinations that cost life savings. Swallowing panic, she considered going home to change. Too late. Back at her elbow was Sidonie.

"You realize he's entertaining some important people tonight," she said. She gave the black-and-red taffeta a pitying look. "I don't suppose you know any of them?"

"As a matter of fact—" March, searching hard, spotted Chen circulating with a tray of glasses. At his heels Noble was performing his starving dog routine. "I know quite a number. Nice party," she told a beaming Chen, helping herself to white wine.

Hunt had unpacked the Czechoslovakian crystal, she noted. Not that she intended to make it any of her business. Where *was* he, anyway? Sidonie was sticking like a burr and any minute she was going to do something desperate.

"I understand you might be staying on to study at Weatherfield University," she heard herself saying.

"Hunter told you, did he? I wasn't planning to, initially. But he can be very persuasive when he wants to."

March fought a losing battle not to be catty. "He

mentioned your broken engagement. I'm sorry. Something like that must be hard to get over.''

Sidonie lowered eloquent eyelashes and said, ''Oh, Hunter's a great help in that department as well. He has this gift for making life seem worth living. Perhaps you've noticed? I remember when I—yes?''

March was spared intimate details by the interruption of a woman in cashmere, saying she was with the Friends of Music and they were absolutely dying to meet the guest of honor. She made her way alone through the living room, aware that she'd been unfair to Sidonie. Hunt did have a gift, and it was for everyone—what made her think she had exclusive rights?

There he was now, in the den, making an older couple laugh with his remarks. Very much the host in fawn slacks and shirt and a silk tie richly patterned in golds and browns. His face, framed against the backdrop of Rene's leather-bound first editions, looked even handsomer if possible than the version she had been carrying about in her head all week.

At the sight of her, he broke off in mid-sentence.

''March! You came!'' he exclaimed, in a tone that made her instantly glad she had. ''Dean? Mrs. Collingwood? Someone special I'd like you to meet. March Briarwood.''

''Delighted.'' Eyes kindly behind rimless spectacles, the dean shook her hand. His wife had upswept hair and a pointed nose.

''How do you do?'' she murmured. ''And what instrument do you play?''

''I don't,'' said March, and retrieved her hand as Hunt explained, laughing, that she didn't have time to play, she was the person who made sure the house survived his lifestyle. And an excellent job she was doing too, as they could see.

"Two pretty young women in residence at The Cedars? Dr. Reynolds, you cunning man! I had no idea you employed a housekeeper—"

Hunt's brow furrowed. He cut the dean's wife short.

"I didn't make myself clear. March isn't my housekeeper. She owns a topflight cleaning service."

"I see. And you were kind enough to invite her to your party." Ada Collingwood gave March's dress a closer inspection. "My dear, you must feel like Cinderella at the ball. I was just saying to Edward earlier, Hunter Reynolds gives the most democratic parties."

"Some cheese to go with your wine, Ada? We mustn't monopolize our host," said the dean. He looked embarrassed as he nudged his wife toward the door. "Bring Ms. Briarwood to tea at my office sometime, won't you, Hunter?"

March didn't know who to feel sorrier for—the dean, or herself, or Hunt. His eyes gleamed with barely suppressed anger.

"My fault. I bungled that one, didn't I?"

She gave a shrug, reminded uncomfortably of Kent. "It comes with the cleaning territory, that kind of attitude. Don't worry about it."

Hunt shook his head. "I didn't ask you here to be insulted. Come on. Let me take you round and introduce you to some of my friends. Sid—" Belatedly, he remembered.

"It's all right. We've already met," she told him coolly. "At the door."

"And?" he prompted.

"She's everything you said, Hunt. I'm looking forward to hearing her play."

"Hmm," he said, eyes narrowed.

She didn't fool him for a minute. All the same, she'd done well, considering she hadn't lied. Sidonie was still with the Friends of Music, being passed from one to another on the far side of the living room like one of Rene's rare art finds on loan. Hunt had gone all out to give the room a festive air, filling in the empty spaces with pink and white azaleas in sumptuous bloom. He'd also removed the protective throws from the sofas and rugs from the carpets, she noted with a twinge of alarm, but she could hardly fault him for that.

"The tall man talking to the woman with fuzzy red hair?" he said, steering her to the group by the credenza. "That's Scott Fielding, a colleague. Sylvie's his wife—you'll like her. She teaches art at the adult education center."

March's smile was strained as they met. Didn't Hunt know any ordinary people, the kind who worked behind counters or taught math? But she needn't have felt intimidated.

Scott grinned disarmingly. "About time! We thought Hunt was going to keep you to himself in that den," he drawled with a wink. Sylvie dimpled and said, "Oh, what a color, that skirt—like raspberry wine!" In no time they were discussing colors.

How nowadays everybody knew what green stood for, and yellow made the sun shine, and the combination of blue and white had a fresh, clean feel to it. Her impression exactly, said March, and found herself describing how she'd come up with the design for the Marchmaids' uniform. The Fieldings were intrigued and Hunt looked proud. It was exactly the tonic she needed to restore her dented self-esteem.

Until Hunt pressed another glass of wine in her hand and said the others would have to excuse them; it wasn't a party until she sampled the buffet.

"Wine and cheese, I thought you said!" exclaimed March, goggling at the dining room table. Jumbo shrimp surrounded by three kinds of dip rose in a pyramid amid lavish cheese boards and baskets of crackers. Ivory tapers burned in Margaret's silver candelabra, highlighting the satisfaction on Hunt's face.

"Impressive, isn't it? I had help, of course."

He moved closer so the couple selecting petits fours at the sideboard with Noble lending encouragement wouldn't overhear. "Kim and Chen have a classmate whose uncle owns a delicatessen. A plate?"

"Thanks."

All this to advance Sidonie's cause. She cut herself a modest wedge of cheese and placed it on a wheat cracker. Unless she was mistaken, that was Margaret's best Belgian lace tablecloth. *And* the Royal Copenhagen platter, resurrected to hold an artistically arranged assortment of fruit that included strawberries out of season.

Hunt intercepted her look.

"The seagull platter wasn't large enough. Besides, ironstone just doesn't cut it in surroundings like these—" He waved a cheese knife in a gesture that took in the French tapestries and the teardrop chandelier and evoked wary glances from the couple at the sideboard.

"Did I say anything?" she hissed.

"No. But I saw you looking. Ditto at the wineglasses earlier."

The couple drifted off and Noble transferred his attentions to Hunt, who tossed him a cube of cheddar. His voice took on a defensive edge. "You didn't expect me to serve sauvignon blanc in plastic cups, did you?"

And jeopardize Sidonie's chances? March bit her lip. "They say too much cheese can make a dog sick."

"Not Noble. He thrives on the stuff. Don't you, big guy?"

Irritation got the better of her. "I suppose Sidonie helped with the preparations. Seeing the party is for her benefit."

"Sid? She had to practice for the performance." His curt rejoinder informed her she was out of line. "And rest. She's not strong yet emotionally. Surely you can understand that?"

They glowered at each other across the shrimp pyramid like hostile strangers. She was beginning to understand a whole lot more than she cared to.

"Discussing the cleanup arrangements, you two?"

Sidonie herself floated into view, attractively framed by the arched doorway. "I hate to interrupt. Only Hunter, isn't it time you set up my harp for me? Some of the guests are looking at their watches."

"Right. We can't have them leave before they get a chance to hear you play." He put down his plate with a swift glance at March. "You'll excuse me? Go and sit with the Fieldings, why don't you?"

She nodded airily, as though it were all one to her. But when he'd left, with Sidonie placing a slim white hand on his arm and saying, "Didn't you see me signaling? Stuck with those Friends! I thought I'd die of boredom," some more of the shine went out of the evening.

Plate in hand, she wandered into the solarium. It

was hopeless—disagreements lurked like sharks under the surface of every conversation she had with Hunt. Fairy lights twinkled among the branches of the bougainvillea. The younger guests had been dancing here, the way she had danced with Hunt, a long time ago it seemed. Now the room was quiet and deserted, except for the chipmunks nibbling at crackers somebody had pushed through the wire of their cage. Scattered applause from the front of the house signaled the start of Sidonie's performance.

March fought back the temptation to stay where she was and offered Four her last strawberry. Skulking in a back room was not the way to keep an eye on the competition.

She squeezed in behind some Friends to hear the end of Hunt's introduction—something flowery about Sidonie Bell being from his favorite part of Canada, and they were in for a rare treat tonight. The cashmere woman shifted to make a space, drawing reproving looks. Hastily March lowered herself onto a hassock.

Craning her neck, she could make out the gold and ivory harp rearing its crowned head in front Margaret's rosy brocade drapes. And Sidonie, with her fair hair shimmering and her skirt falling over her knees like an inverted lily cup. A sigh rustled through the audience as she touched her hands to the strings.

Music cascaded into the room, notes sparkling and clear as drops of water in the sun. March wondered guiltily how it was possible to dislike anyone who could coax such sounds from an instrument. As the piece ended and a Celtic folk song full of wistful wanting took its place, she stole a glance at Hunt.

He was leaning against the wall behind the dean's chair, arms folded. She could tell from his profile that he was listening raptly. When the final chord died away, he stepped forward and drew Sidonie to her feet to a storm of applause.

She smiled up at him. Even from the back of the room, it was impossible to mistake the nature of the emotion in her lovely face.

March tiptoed across the atrium and into the den. Closing the door behind her didn't help. She could still hear the triumphant encore that followed. She stared at Rene's first editions through a haze of tears, unable to deny the tide of self-doubt any longer.

She should have known better than to come. Dressed like a cocktail waitress at an upscale evening for a lot of brainy and artistic people—she was out of her depth. Being an expert on cleaning houses was *not* the same as being an expert at making music. When had a shiny floor ever touched a man's heart the way a polished performance did? She started for the door, went back for the clutch bag she'd left lying on the coffee table earlier, and, turning, almost collided with Hunt.

"March, I saw you leave. What's wrong?"

"Nothing."

She avoided his eyes. "It's been a long day and I'm tired. I thought this would be a good time to slip out and go home."

"Just like that? Without a word? Not even goodbye?" He placed his hands on her shoulders and peered into her face. "You've been crying! March, what is it?"

"The music got to me, I guess." She managed a tremulous smile. "Sidonie really does play divinely. Shouldn't you be with her?"

"Forget Sid! She doesn't need me anymore. The

dean's showering her with compliments and the rest of the room is lined up, waiting to." His expression darkened. "Has Ada Collingwood been making remarks again?"

"No. And even if she had—" She couldn't stop her shoulders from giving a sad little shrug. "—Mrs. Collingwood only calls things as she sees them."

"Aren't you forgetting something?" His hand came up to tilt her chin. "Cinderella was a princess. Doesn't matter what the others thought. The prince knew, the minute he laid eyes on her."

Their glances met and her breathing stilled. "How did he?"

"Simple. She was the most beautiful woman at the ball."

March flushed and looked at her skirt. "If you're referring to the way I'm dressed, maybe Cinderella should have worn slacks and a sweater the same as everybody else." Well, nearly everybody. Sidonie Bell wore lily-garb.

"What for? You aren't the same as everybody else."

Hunt's gaze traveled downward, over the creamy expanse of her throat and the lilting curves of her bodice, and his tone took on a husky quality. "You could wear your work apron and you'd look like a princess. March, two months we've known each other, and you still can't tell how I see you?"

She shook her head, hungry for the reassurance that only he could give, and as though he read her mind, he drew her into his arms.

"Come here. There's just one sure way I know to tell you," he murmured, and lowering his mouth to hers, he kissed her.

"Oh," she whispered. She tingled all over.

She slid her arms around his waist and held him close as he repeated the kiss with variations. A slow warmth expanded inside her, crowding out doubt and fear, arguments, even Sidonie herself, until she and Hunt were all that mattered—

Noise filtered through her consciousness. Feet running, a woman screaming. March broke off the kiss. "Hunt, your guests—"

He groaned. "What the devil?" he muttered, and started for the door.

Some kind of riot appeared to be under way. People rushed in all directions, shrieking and laughing. Noble added his bark from somewhere. Crossing the atrium, March was almost knocked down by a Friend brandishing an umbrella. Hunt slipped a protective arm around her.

"Will somebody tell me what's going on here?" he roared.

Kim materialized, his glasses askew. "Professor Reynolds! The chipmunks—somebody opened the cage. They are every place—"

"The chipmunks! Is that all?" Hunt started to laugh, but checked himself at the sight of the cushion in Kim's hand. "You weren't using that to—"

"Not me! Mrs. Dean. I take it from her. Chipmunk One? He climb the pantleg of Mr. Dean—" His explanation was cut short when a small furry shape streaked over the tiles with Noble in pursuit, big paws skidding as he attempted to round the fountain.

Hunt lunged and grabbed the dog by the collar. "Kim! Find Chen and Professor Fielding," he ordered. "Then get me the fishing net from the garage. March?" He paused to wrestle with Noble, who detected a rustling in the gloxinias. "Down, boy! March—could you—possibly—shut him up somewhere?"

She succeeded in dragging the dog to the laundry room. Recklessly she promised him more cheese later and hurried back to the atrium. A number of guests were leaving, bundling themselves into their coats, among them the dean and his wife.

Ada Collingwood's face was the color of ripe cherries.

"It's like a students' dormitory in here. Worse!" she snapped, glaring at March.

"That's the trouble with democratic parties," said March politely, seeing them to the door.

She thought the dean smiled. Where was Sidonie, and why wasn't she doing the honors? In the living room, Hunt admonished the remaining guests to stay calm. "They're harmless. Unless provoked," he amended with a glance at March. "The less yelling and rushing around we do, the better our chances of catching them."

He called for volunteers and organized them into teams, one for each escapee. Scott Fielding's team cornered its quarry almost immediately. Number Three had taken refuge under the rosewood wall unit; the problem was how to flush him out?

"A broom!" a voice suggested.

"You'll scare him! Try food," cried Sylvie, and cashews were sprinkled on the carpet while Scott held a tipped-over wastebasket at the ready.

March sighed. Cashews were the least of the litter underfoot. Crackers, ground-in cheese, and next to the coffee table, blush pink roses amid shattered shards of crystal. "I thought we'd packed away the good vases," she grumbled, on her hands and knees.

Hunt, his eyes on a chipmunk inspecting a coffee cup, overheard her. As she'd meant him to.

"What did you want me to use? A yogurt tub?" He sounded amused. Exhilarated, in fact. Picking up a lace table runner, he centered it over the cup.

Potted azaleas weren't enough for Sidonie, oh no, a party for her required roses—ouch! March pricked her finger, going after a shard too aggressively. The chipmunk reared up on tiny hind legs, and a white cloud descended over his head. A squeak of protest, and he'd been rolled into a neat package to be handed over to Chen.

"One down and three to go!" exclaimed Hunt with a wink at March.

He was enjoying this—in his element, by the look of it.

"Two down!" echoed the team at the wall unit, as Scott slid a magazine under the upended basket and an outraged scrabbling sounded from inside.

March salvaged what she could of the roses. It was all too easy to picture Hunt on one of his wildlife field trips. Maybe that's what he was doing, too. Imagining himself back in the wilds and realizing what he'd been missing. The thought was sharper than broken glass. Shouts rose as chipmunk One burst into the room and scrambled up a drape. Perched on top of the valance, whiskers twitching and paws pressed against his tawny vest, he contemplated his pursuers.

A woman said "How sweet!" and everybody laughed, including Hunt.

March turned to him in a temper. "Do something, can't you? He's making holes in the brocade. Next he'll be jumping on the harp. Where's Sidonie, anyway? Why isn't she looking after her property?''

"The commotion was giving her a headache.'' Hunt's tone was bland. ''I suggested she go somewhere quiet and relax.''

Kim arrived with the net and March held her breath while Hunt maneuvered it into position. At least away on field trips he'd be out of Sidonie's range. But out of hers, too, so that thought was cold comfort. A gasp went up: Hunt had missed. One scurried down the other drape and headed for the dining room, tail hoisted like a banner, and his audience surged after him, bowling over a luckless azalea plant. March's hand flew to her mouth.

Standing by the table was Sidonie. She screamed and dropped a plate. One leaped for the safety of the nearest hanging object, which happened to be her skirt. Swaying, he launched himself at the tablecloth just as Sidonie, with perfect timing, collapsed into Hunt's outstretched arms.

"He came right at me! It was awful. Those little rat's feet!''

Moaning, she buried her head on his shoulder, while Hunt made soothing noises and stroked her hair. Everybody crowded round, commiserating; Scott poured her a glass of sherry. March exchanged glances with Sylvie—evidently they'd been struck by the same thought. Why was it, men could never tell theatrics from the real thing when a pretty woman was involved? Checking the table, she saw that One had recovered his aplomb and was stuffing his pouched cheeks with grapes.

Poised directly overhead, in the hands of Chen, was the net.

"Chen? Wait! I don't think that's—"

Too late! The net descended and One, equipped with eyes in the back of his sleek head, took a running jump at the sideboard. Half a dozen Czechoslovakian wineglasses skidded and crashed. After that, everything occured in slow motion.

Swinging the net around, Chen managed to entangle the handle in the lace tablecloth. March had barely time to snatch up the candelabra before assorted baskets and bowls, and finally the Royal Copenhagen platter itself, were carried along to the brink of the table and sailed majestically to the floor. Where, predictably, the platter smashed.

Eventually, Hunt got everybody to go home.

Everybody except March. "You'll stay?" he asked, his eyes full of undisguised pleading.

"Lifesaver," he'd murmured appreciatively in her ear when, against her better judgement, she'd agreed.

Now he was in the solarium, settling the overexcited chipmunks down for the night. He'd make a great father. Assuming some woman was foolhardy enough to take him on. At the moment, March wasn't sure she still wanted to try. She put Kim and Chen in charge of the dishwasher, tied a towel around her waist, and returned to the dining room to sweep up the debris and hopefully perform magic on the dip stains setting in the carpet.

Sidonie drooped against the sideboard, sipping a second sherry.

"How was I supposed to know, One would come in here? I was feeling faint and thought some food would help. The dean was *that* close to telling me I was accepted! Now all he'll remember is those horrid beasts rampaging around the house scaring people to death.''

"They were only chipmunks. Not grizzlies," March pointed out. If she had to listen to Sidonie much longer, she'd scream. "Maybe if you'd pitch in and help clean up, it would take your mind off things."

"You've got to be kidding! My big evening ruined, my head splitting, and you're suggesting I clean?" The golden lashes fell. "Anyway, that's your line of work. Not mine."

March gritted her teeth. "My job has nothing to do with helping out tonight. I was invited to this party as Hunt's guest. The same as you."

"You actually believe that?" Sidonie's laugh tinkled like a cool little bell. "Use your common sense, March. Our situations at The Cedars are nowhere near the same."

March squirted more shampoo on the carpet and swabbed vigorously. "All the more reason to think you'd want to try to repay him. After everything he's done for you!"

"I wouldn't worry my head about it, if I were you. There are better ways of repaying a man besides down on your knees cleaning for him. Didn't Hunter tell you, he had this terrific crush on me when we lived next door to each other?" Sidonie shook back her hair in a self-satisfied gesture. "Merely because we're older now and went our separate ways, doesn't mean I've forgotten how to make him happy."

March opened her mouth, then snapped it shut. Kim, carrying a tray of used glasses, paused beside her. "Ms. Briarwood? Sorry to tell you. But Noble is sick in the living room. On the carpet behind the second sofa."

"Oh, no!" She sank back on her heels—the absolute final straw!

"Too much cheese, it looks like," said Kim. "I'll get the paper towels."

Sidonie's glance was pitying.

"Your sister and brother-in-law would be livid if they knew. I can't say I'd blame them. Well . . ." She yawned delicately. "If Hunter's looking for me, let him know I've taken his advice and gone to bed, will you?"

When he returned from the solarium, March was noisily gathering up cleaning equipment.

"Persuaded Sid to get some rest, did you?" he observed cheerfully. "You're a wonder, March, you really are! Tonight would have been a disaster without you. I don't know how I could have coped."

She stared at him, trying to recall how she'd felt when he kissed her, but the only person she could picture in his arms was Sidonie.

"Sure. Take the worry out of partying. Invite a Marchmaid and let the good times roll."

His smile faded. "Hey, wait a minute. You're not implying it's my fault the chipmunks got loose and Chen was careless?"

"Isn't it?" Gloomily she eyed a strawberry under the sideboard where she couldn't reach. "Oh, not directly. You didn't unlock the cage. You didn't smash the crystal or drop the dip. But you're the reason The Cedars is full of stuff that doesn't belong. Wildlife, the dog. Parties that get out of hand. It's the way you live, Hunt—that's what's to blame."

"Really."

He was angry now, as angry as she, judging by the thunderclouds building in his face. "That's what matters to you, isn't it? Making sure the carpets aren't violated. The crockery isn't manhandled. Heck, I wouldn't be surprised if concern for the house is the reason you accepted my invitation at all!''

''Hunt! That's not true.'' Her voice balked at the image of herself he'd presented. ''I'm saying there has to be a middle ground. If you'd exercise a little restraint. A little care—''

''I do. It's the people who live here I care about. Whether they're happy and productive—''

''Sidonie. You're talking about Sidonie Bell, aren't you?''

''Yes, Sid. And the boys. Me! March, I thought we'd been through all this.''

''Not quite all of it,'' she said, dragging off her makeshift apron and tossing it at his feet. It was pointless to argue with a man determined not to see her side. ''You told me Sidonie had a crush on you. You neglected to mention that you had one on her. Did it conveniently slip your mind?''

He flushed under his tan. ''That was years ago. We were both kids! It's not worth discussing—''

''Sidonie thinks it is. In fact, she discussed more than that. She took pains to inform me that she still knows how to make you happy.''

''And you believe her?'' He sounded shocked.

She tossed her head.

''Shouldn't I? You're not kids now and Sidonie is as much in love with you as ever.'' She started for the atrium, heels tapping shakily over the marble. ''It was in her face for the whole room to see when she finished playing. Ask anybody. They'll say you didn't look exactly indifferent either, showing off your big star.''

"That's fantasy. Strictly in your head! Maybe it's what you want to believe." He caught up with her, his tread firm and accusing. "Maybe because it's easier than having faith in yourself. Or having faith in a man who doesn't live, and doesn't behave, the way you think he should!"

She clapped her hands over her ears to block out the hateful truth of what she heard. But she had to lower them to get into her coat, and anyway, his voice had risen to a level that probably reached all the way back to the bedrooms. She could almost see the smile curving Sidonie's lips.

"Maybe you should send me a bill for tonight!" he shouted. "Keep everything between us on a business level. Cut out the messy emotions. The misunderstandings."

"All right, if that's what you want. In fact, I'll do better than that!" she cried, yanking at the heavy oak door.

He didn't try to stop her. The last thing she saw before she turned to run down the steps was his hurt, hostile face.

Chapter Nine

"You're sending them back? All of them?" Anna Rose looked up from the week's schedule with her face mirroring disbelief. "March, you can't be serious!"

"No? Watch me."

March spun the dial of the safe and carried the envelope marked VERMEER back to the desk. She'd had the whole of Sunday to think it over. "Returning the postdated checks will be a wake-up call. My last hope of making Hunt Reynolds realize he can't keep on living the way he is at The Cedars." *And he can't have both me and Sidonie either,* she added mentally. Unfortunately there was nothing she could send back to make that clear.

She reached for an envelope engraved with the Marchmaids logo and wrote his name and The Cedars address in bold letters, aware of Anna Rose's troubled gaze on her. She had told her a lot about the party Saturday night, but not everything. Some of the details were too humiliating to remember, let alone repeat.

"And if Hunt calls your bluff? Tears up the checks and decides The Cedars can do without us?"

"I'm gambling it won't come to that. But it's a chance I'll have to take."

Anna Rose bent over her papers. "Not the best of

timing. With all the customers we lost to CleanRight last week.''

''I know. I know!'' March put down her pen and turned tired eyes on her friend. ''But I can't go on like this. All Hunt and I do is argue. Over the wineglasses, the animals, his friends . . .'' Old female friends, specifically. ''Besides which, Bettina refuses flat out to work there anymore.''

''Because of Sidonie Bell, you mean?'' The entire staff knew about the clash of wills between Bettina and Hunt's guest; it ranked right after the CleanRight franchise as topic of the month in the change room. ''How much longer is that woman going to be around, anyway?''

''Forever maybe.'' If Sidonie had her way, which seemed a definite possibity. ''Apparently the dean was in raptures over her playing.''

Anna Rose put a question mark in The Cedars' time slot. ''And Margaret and Rene?'' she said carefully. ''What are you going to tell them if Hunt does drop us?''

March was ready for that one. She smiled without humor. ''I'll let Hunt do the explaining. That should test his ingenuity.'' She pulled a blank sheet of stationery toward her and wrote, *Best for both of us under the circumstances. I'm sure you'll agree.* Staring at the words, she felt desolate. How could something that hurt so much, be best for anybody? She surreptitiously rubbed a hand over her cheeks.

''You're crying. Oh, March!'' Anna Rose passed her a box of tissues from the top of the filing cabinet. ''I'm so sorry!''

''*You're* sorry!'' She blew her nose. ''If I'd listened to you and not let myself fall for the big bear, this

wouldn't be happening." She folded her note around
the checks and stuffed them into the envelope. "I'll
drop these in a mailbox on my way to the dealer's.
The sooner they're gone, the sooner I can get on with
my life," she said. A trite phrase that didn't fool either
of them.

Anna Rose hovered in the hall while she put on her
raincoat. "You never did tell me. What happened to
the fourth chipmunk?"

"Kim found him in the kitchen. Rolled up asleep
in a cashew tin."

"Little beasts must have been terrified!"

"They didn't act it. As far as I could see they were
having a rousing good time. Same as everybody else."
She frowned. Almost everybody else. "Before I forget. Better take these home tonight." She felt in her
pocket and pulled out the velvet box. "And thanks
again. They were lovely."

"But not lucky," said Anna Rose sadly. "Don't
you think you should send those checks registered?"

She was right. Trust Anna Rose to be prudent, even
when the world was falling apart! Besides, the return
of the checks would have more impact if Hunt had to
sign for them.

March handed the clerk at the counter her envelope
and watched it, duly stamped, disappear into the inner
workings of the post office with a bleak sense of
watching bridges burn. Didn't the weather do anything
pleasant anymore? she wondered, unfurling her umbrella against a spate of raindrops in the parking lot.

A cello-wrapped florist's package sat waiting on the
steps for her when she got home.

Inside was a pot of blue hyacinths, the delicate bells
poised to open. Hyacinths in October! Her pulse

quickening, she leaned against the kitchen counter to read the card tucked in among the silvery green. *Sorry* was written on it, and Hunt's signature.

She touched his name with her fingertips, as if through the script she could touch the man. Just *sorry.* For what? she mused, hardening her heart as she tidied away the wrappings and went to place the pot on her desk. For the accusations he'd made? For Sidonie's rudeness? For the fact that their relationship hadn't worked out? March groaned aloud. If it wasn't dead yet, it certainly would be once he laid eyes on the checks.

The hyacinths went from bud to showy bloom, with a fragrance that filled the house. Thea, whose niece worked in a flower shop, said they must have been ordered specially from Toronto. A crease appeared between Anna Rose's brows every time she looked at them.

"He's trying to tell you something. They're the exact same shade as your eyes."

March tossed her head. Haunting her, was what he was doing. She woke up at night to the smell of hyacinths and the fleeting feel of his arms around her.

Hunt telephoned on Wednesday while she was out.

Anna Rose greeted her with the news when she returned from distributing flyers. "Your letter arrived, and is he ever mad!" she called up from the basement.

"He's supposed to be." March stood at the top of the stairs. Mad enough to transform his lifestyle? "What did he say?"

"That you should know by now he can't manage without you." Anna Rose appeared, face upturned over an armful of dust cloths. "He can see why you were upset. Only he doesn't think it's fair of you to hold one evening against him."

One evening! As if that were all. And was that her he couldn't manage without, or Marchmaids? "What is he going to do about it?"

"He didn't say. Except that he's hoping you'll reconsider. Oh, and to tell you he's ordered a new platter. But he can't find a store that stocks that particular design of wineglass, and can you suggest one?"

"They don't make that design anymore and no, I can't." What about her heart? she felt like shouting. He'd broken that, too, and she couldn't simply run out and get a replacement. "The nerve!"

"Does that mean you're not going to?"

"Reconsider? No! Whose side are you on, anyway?"

"Well, excuse *me!*" Anna Rose disappeared and March heard the lid of the washing machine slam shut. "Sometimes I don't understand you, March. I thought that was the object of the exercise. To give the man another chance."

"He makes it sound as though he's giving us the chance." She shut her eyes and leaned her forehead against the doorjamb. Anna Rose was worried about the dwindling customers and her job—they all were. More quietly, she said, "Did he mention Sidonie Bell?"

"No."

"Then what's the point? The staff won't put up with her." The staff was only an excuse, she thought. *I'm the one who won't go back, as long as Sidonie is at The Cedars.* The washing machine clanked and churned, and Anna Rose's face reappeared.

"So what do I tell him about cleaning? Just leave him hanging?"

March kicked off her pumps and started up the stairs to her bedroom. She must have hit every apartment lobby and supermarket bulletin board within miles with her flyers. "Tell him to try CleanRight, if you care so much," she said. "I'm going to soak my feet."

Margaret would understand. She had to. She'd fought, too, in her way, for Rene. Going back to college to take evening art courses, buying designer clothes when they couldn't really afford either.

For the rest of the week she and Anna Rose tiptoed around the subject of Hunt like a patch of soapy water. Saturday, March was ambushed by guilt watching Bettina and Jamie load up their hatchback. At the last minute, Jamie came running back into the office.

"Forgot the address for this new place you're sending us," he explained. Something in March's face as she handed it to him made him pause.

"It's not the same, is it? Without The Cedars on a Saturday morning?"

Mutely, she shook her head.

"I don't care what Bettina says, I miss the place. Sure, it was lots of work, but it was never dull."

March nodded; the lump in her throat made speaking difficult. Jamie looked back from the door, his face shy. "Excuse me butting in, Ms. Briarwood. But I sure hope you and the professor can iron things out between you."

She hoped so, too—he had no idea how much! For the first time she wondered if she'd been too hasty, too inflexible. She stared after Jamie as he accelerated down the driveway with the self-assurance common to nineteen-year-olds. Strange, how self-assurance flew out the window when you fell in love.

The weekend was endless. Looking up from a desk piled with bills Sunday at the blue sky blazing behind the lipstick plant, she wondered if she was becoming one of those people Hunt had warned her about—only good for work. The Weatherfield Fair was in progress and for a while she wandered about the grounds, staring at the prize milkers with their big mournful eyes and the trestle tables laden with homemade chutney and apple pies. She couldn't honestly say she was enjoying herself.

"Come back and teach me how, Hunt," she whispered, under cover of the nostalgic little waltz on the carousel. "I can't do it alone."

Next day there was a message on the answering machine.

He didn't think much of her tip, announced Hunt dryly. CleanRight had arrived late and left early. They'd been sloppy with the vacuuming, locked out the dog, and lost some essays off his desk. Worse still, he'd discovered a chip in Margaret's art nouveau mirror that he could swear wasn't there before.

March felt happier than she had in days. "Forgive me, Maggie," she whispered. Quickly, before she lost her nerve, she left an answering message. "Could I quote you on that? It sounds exactly like what my customers need to hear."

She was in the shower the next time he called and she missed the sound of the bell. When she switched on the machine, he said, "Feel free. Did you get the flowers I sent?"

It was a start, she thought. They were talking again. Just. She picked a time when she was sure he'd be in class before she dialed again. "Yes, I got them. Very nice. But are they supposed to make everything all right?"

It was like starting over, she thought. The two of them trading provocations on each other's machines. She had to wait a couple of days for the next installment and for a while she worried she'd lost him. Or Anna Rose had gotten to the machine first and erased something to spare her feelings. Once she dreamed Hunt was standing before her with open arms, only the figure that came to fill them was Sidonie's, blond hair shimmering. When she awoke, her face was wet with tears.

The telephone rang while she was getting ready for bed Friday night, and she froze—what if the dream had been an omen? Like a coward she was going to let the machine take the call, only after the third ring she couldn't stand the suspense and picked up the receiver.

"March? Thank heaven! I'll be right over."

He hung up before she could say a word. She pulled her kimono on over her nightdress and went downstairs to turn on some lights. Possibilities swirled in her head. Sidonie had left in a huff. He and Sid were eloping and could she see about getting a new house sitter? Kim or Chen had had an accident. By the time the Range Rover pulled up in the drive she was prepared for anything.

"Hunt, what on earth—"

"Sorry. I know it's late."

His eyes were solicitous as he followed her into the kitchen. "I think you'd better sit down," he suggested, and that was already enough to keep her standing. "Those paintings in the bedroom corridor," he said. "They were from the Group of Seven?"

"Two of them. The other—" The hanging lamp over the table swayed. " 'Were,' did you say?"

"March, I don't know an easy way to tell you this. There's been a break-in at The Cedars."

She gasped. It was the one eventuality she hadn't considered.

"Earlier tonight while I was out. The thieves didn't take much. Probably because most of the good stuff's packed away. Aside from the paintings, only Saint Francis as far as I know . . ."

Only! March wondered if this was another dream— a nightmare, actually. "Didn't the alarm go off? Where were the boys? Sid?"

"The house was empty. Professionals, apparently. They managed to deactivate the alarm. The police are checking into it." He frowned at her expression. "Francis is covered by insurance, surely?"

"Everything is. But that carving is Margaret's favorite. The police are there now?"

"Yes. They thought it would be helpful if you came back with me. To confirm what was taken. Since I'm merely the tenant . . ."

"Of course." Something in his tone alerted her. "They're not thinking *you* had something to do with it?"

"An inside job, you mean?" His grin didn't quite reach his eyes. "It crossed their minds. Till we got Dean Collingwood on the phone and he vouched for me."

March didn't know at what point she'd sunk into a chair but abruptly, she stood up. "Wait here. I'll be with you as soon as I put some clothes on."

"Thanks. Two character references never hurt. And March?" His eyes held her at the foot of the stairs. The gleam in his pupils wasn't gratitude. "Before you change?"

"Yes?"

"Nice. That dressing gown you're wearing."

"Oh." She looked down at herself and in the nick of time refrained from blurting out, "This old thing?" She was glad she did because what he said next was, "The color matches your eyes. Like the hyacinths."

She ran upstairs, propelled by a surge of warm feeling that went a long way to dispel the numbing cold of the news he'd brought. Jeans, runners, a fleecy gray sweatshirt—she dug things out of the closet at random and threw them on. They'd have to call Rene and Margaret, much as she hated to. She found the telephone number of their hotel in Brussels in her night table and slipped it into a pocket, imagining Margaret's face going white with shock when she told her. What struck her as astonishing was that Hunt, Sidonie, the boys, and apparently even the dog, had all managed to be out of the house at the same time.

"The others don't live at The Cedars anymore, that's why. They've moved out. Gone home. Relocated. Noble and the chipmunks, too." She had waited till they were in the Range Rover before asking. Now Hunt's eyes met hers sidelong in the light from the dashboard.

"I was planning to tell you tomorrow," he said. "Over a bottle of champagne with maybe a trumpet voluntary in the background after I got you to come over and see for yourself."

"Good heavens!"

Her brain felt blank. Nothing could be as big a

shock as news of the break-in, she'd thought, but she was wrong. "When did this happen?" she asked.

"Over the course of the week." He paused, waiting for green at the intersection. "Noble was the last and he left this afternoon. Obviously the thieves were watching. Anyway, I was at the university. A department meeting that ran late. When I got back, all the windows were lit up and the front door was standing open."

"Hunt! You didn't go inside?"

She felt a sudden urge to touch him, to assure herself that he was whole and safe. Her skin crawled when she thought of what might have happened to him—never mind Saint Francis.

"Not right away. First I called 911 from my car phone. By then it was pretty clear the house was empty."

The lights were still on as they pulled up in the driveway behind two police cruisers. March shivered again as they started up the walk. Nerves, not cold, she decided, grateful for the sensation of Hunt's arm snug around her shoulders.

"It'll be all right," he said. "You'll see."

As soon as they were inside, going from one room to another, she started to feel better. She had half expected vandalism and she'd been afraid to ask, but there was none. Everything looked normal, except for the police officers everywhere. A silver-haired man glanced up from his tape measure in the corridor under the skylights and started toward them.

"Detective Sergeant Ryan?" said Hunt. "March Briarwood. Mrs. Vermeer's sister."

"Good of you to come," he said, and flipped open his notepad. He had a seamed, clever face. "Before we get to the pieces that were taken, if you would just answer a few other questions for us?''

''Anything. If I can.''

''Know him well, do you? Professor Reynolds here?''

When it was over and the police had left, the house seemed more silent and empty than she had ever experienced it.

''Coffee?'' said Hunt. ''Unless you're in a hurry to get back.''

She accompanied him to the kitchen. ''I don't think I could sleep.''

''Thanks for the vote of confidence back there.''

''I only told the truth. Luckily being hospitable isn't a crime.''

''Only a complication,'' he observed. He had his back to her, rummaging in the cupboard for the coffee tin.

''Yes.'' She sighed. ''Although you couldn't tell from looking at the place now.'' All the surfaces were bare as though nobody lived here anymore. No pizza boxes or computer printouts or discarded gym shoes messing up the rooms, no cups with lipstick rims, not a single one of the chewed-up tennis balls Noble was forever carrying home. She glanced at Hunt in sudden apprehension.

''You didn't send Noble to the animal shelter, did you?''

''Would you care?'' He measured out spoonfuls of coffee. Relenting, he said, ''Of course not. The Fieldings live out in the country. They have two dogs of their own and Sylvie said, what was one more?''

She nodded, trying not to feel guilty. In the solarium

156

Ingrid Betz

there'd been a gaping space behind the Norfolk Island pine.

"And the chipmunks? What did you do with them?"

"Took them to Riverview Café and let them go near a hollow log. They were old enough and certainly fat enough—after the gorging they did at the party—to survive the winter."

A little stab went through her when he said Riverview Café, and all the sunny pleasure of that afternoon came flooding back. The first-time-ever sensation of Hunt's lips on hers, the seductive way his hand had moved down her back. She straightened her spine and went to stand in the dining room arch. Even the dip stains on the carpet had vanished, she noted.

"CleanRight did that?" she asked.

"Are you kidding? I did. Somebody in the chemistry lab told me what to use."

"A formula, you mean?"

"Magic. Club soda and baking soda."

"Really!" She hadn't known that. She turned. The coffee was burbling now, filling the kitchen with fragrance. He set mugs on the table and the matching sugar and creamer and she thought how dexterous his big, square-tipped fingers were and how they had felt on her skin that day under the poplars.

"You cover the stain with baking soda," he said, "pour the liquid over, and let soak. It turns a funny murky green and a few hours later the whole thing washes out . . ." His voice slowed and stopped.

"Amazing," she breathed.

She couldn't seem to disentangle her gaze from his, or perhaps it was the other way around. A pleasurable tide of confusion threatened to engulf her. "That's . . . a useful tip to know," she stammered.

Amusement crinkled the corners of his eyes.

"Maybe it'll give Marchmaids the edge they need." Not amusement only, she thought with a catch in her throat—affection, too, and more.

"Hunt?" She had to know. "What made you change your mind? Get everybody to move out?"

"Do you really need to ask?" He gave a lopsided grin that made her heart ache. "I finally did some serious thinking. About what I was doing to the house and how unfair it was to the people concerned. Rene, Margaret. You, caught in the middle! I guess the real eye-opener was the way things spun out of control the night of the party. Good intentions were no excuse. The animals and the boarders had to go."

March sat warily on a chair. "And Sidonie Bell? Did she have to go, too?" That was the question at the heart of everything.

Hunt reached for the coffeepot and poured. He looked sheepish. "Sid—now there's a whole other story."

"Didn't Dean Collingwood want her in the course, after all?"

"Oh, he wanted her! Only Sid decided she preferred the climate in B.C." He handed March a steaming mug. Grinning, he said, "You'd be surprised, how chilly it got in here after you left. Cream and sugar?"

She nodded and he pushed them across to her before straddling the chair opposite. "And that's another apology I owe you." He shook his head, a man who didn't know how he could have been so blind. "Sid was waiting for me in my room, if you can believe it."

March flushed. She could believe it.

"Said she was still upset and needed some tender loving care. The kind only I could provide. 'Rekindling the embers' was a phrase she used. I'm afraid I wasn't very diplomatic." Hunt frowned into his mug. "I had her packed and at the airport, harp and five suitcases, in time for the Sunday-morning flight to Vancouver."

March let out a long silent breath, the one she seemed to have been holding for the last two weeks.

"Poor Sidonie." Easy enough to be compassionate now that the threat was removed. "So there were no sparks left?" she asked in a neutral tone.

He fixed reproachful eyes on her. "Did you honestly imagine there would be?"

She lowered her lashes. "How could I know? A lovely creature like Sidonie! You cared for her once—"

"Sure, I spent some time with her. Why not? I was a normal youthful male. But I discovered fast, cool blond angels aren't my cup of tea when it comes to romance. It made me furious to think she had you believing otherwise."

March sighed. "I think it was her talent, more than her looks or the things she said, that persuaded me," she confessed. He leaned forward, a hint of anger surfacing in his eyes.

"What about *your* talent? Turning disaster areas into gracious homes! Musicians have their place, I'll be the first to admit, but what this planet needs is more people to keep it clean and habitable. Indoors as well as out."

She laughed and pushed back her chair. Nice of him to say so, although she wasn't entirely convinced. Automatically she picked up their mugs and carried them to the sink. Hunt took them gently out of her hands and turned off the tap. ''No,'' he said. ''I may admire what you can do, but I'm never again going to take it for granted.''

He stood very close and his gaze seemed even closer. It was a long time since he had looked at her in that essential male way. She had been so afraid he never would again.

His arms slid around her and she felt herself warming, melting, going up like tinder as he moved against her and whispered into her hair, ''You could stay. Now that the night's half over. Why hurry home?''

Why indeed? If there was a reason, she had forgotten it. In her mind she was already his, body and soul. This time when they kissed, there would be no halfway, no turning back with her emotions.

''Shouldn't we call Rene and Margaret first? With the time difference we can catch them at breakfast. Later on, they'll be gone for the day.''

He grimaced. He was as close to going up in flames as she. ''You're right. Have you got the number?''

To his credit, he did most of the talking. March could tell he felt badly, as though he'd let Rene down. Although as Rene assured her when Hunt passed her the phone, ''I'm thankful nobody was in the house to get hurt. Besides, the loss could have been greater. If the two of you hadn't packed things away . . .''

''But Saint Francis! I know how Margaret doted on him.''

''Very stupid of the thieves. The piece is unique. It'll be recognized the instant they try to sell it.''

They'd book the next available flight home, he said firmly; there'd be paperwork to deal with for the insurance. "I think Rene's secretly relieved to be going back to the gallery," put in Margaret. "He didn't have much confidence in the temporary manager."

"You said the same thing about Hunt, remember?"

"And? Was I wrong?"

"Wrong and right, both. I've missed you, Maggie." The old name slipped out and for once it didn't earn March a reprimand.

"What was that about me being wrong and right?" Hunt wanted to know when she'd replaced the receiver.

"Not you. Margaret," she teased. His hand was around her waist, warm and insistent, and it took no words at all for them to start moving down the sky-lit corridor. The walls looked bare but what she missed even more than the paintings was Chen bowling tennis balls here for Noble. She couldn't help saying, "Funny, how lifeless the house seems with nobody in it."

He slanted her a look down his nose. "You noticed."

"Yes." She paused. "It is possible—I was wrong about some things."

"Really? That's not the message I got when you returned the checks."

She flinched at his tone, aware of the hurt she must have inflicted to cause it. What could she say? "I hope at least Kim and Chen moved somewhere decent. Not back to that awful apartment."

"As if I'd let them! Their classmate's uncle rented them a couple of rooms above the deli. Meals thrown in free." They stopped and Hunt turned to face her, shoulders hunched and fists plunged in his pockets. "Kim told me, what Sid said to you after the party.

He was pretty mad—the boys think you're one fine lady.''

March's cheeks grew warm. ''They're nice people.'' Nicer than Sidonie, but he knew that now, so what was the point of going on about it? Through an open door she saw Hunt's bed, with the sleeping bag laid out neatly on top, and she knew that if there was ever a moment to be completely honest with him, it was now.

''About the checks. Hunt, I was desperate.'' Her eyes willed him to understand the fear that had gnawed at her. ''I didn't know anymore whether it was me you wanted. Or Marchmaids.''

He stared at her, and for a minute she thought, *Now I've offended him.* Then his eyes began to dance.

''I will admit—'' He straightened up and drew his hands out of his pockets. ''There were times. When I might have let you think it was Marchmaids. Simply because it was the only way I could be absolutely sure of seeing you again.''

She leaned against the doorjamb and took an unsteady breath. ''I guess, one way and another, we've both been pretty blind.''

''And pretty stubborn,'' he murmured, focusing his attention on her lips. In one fluid movement, he tipped her chin upward in his palm and captured her trembling mouth with his own, warm and sweet. He pulled her into his arms and all the pent-up hunger of weeks was in his kiss, all the urgency and passion she had dreamed of and more. When he raised his head at last to look at her, tears were rolling down her cheeks. He took his thumb and brushed them away with rough gentleness.

"The last time, I swear. That you have to cry on my account."

"I'm not crying." She smiled at his blurred face. "This is happiness. Can't you tell?"

She reached for his hand and placed it where he could feel her heart pounding through the soft fabric of her shirt. Longing suffused his face.

"We've got to talk," he murmured. His lips feathered kisses on her earlobe, the pulse in her throat. Tantalizing. Promising. "Rene and Margaret will be back in a few days."

She nodded and he said, "That doesn't give us much time."

"Time?"

"Before I leave. I'm only the house sitter here, remember?"

"You're moving, you mean. To a place of your own."

"I'll be leaving Weatherfield. To go back to B.C." Frowning, he propped himself on one elbow. "March? I thought you realized."

Chapter Ten

March struggled upright with a panicky feeling.

"Well, yes. Eventually. I realized that. But right away? What about your class? I thought you'd been hired to lecture for a full term."

"That was the deal. But they're doing some re-shuffling in the department—that's what the meeting was about. So I had a choice to make and one of them was leaving now."

"I see." She didn't ask what the other choice was, since he'd obviously made up his mind. "How convenient for you!"

She straightened her clothes and smoothed her hair. The dreadful vulnerable feeling was back. What had she been thinking of? Allowing herself to come *this* close, when she knew the type of man Hunt was! A strange, wanton-looking woman arrested her glance in the dresser mirror. Flushed cheeks, enormous eyes, hair a silky tangle. Over her shoulder she saw Hunt agitatedly run fingers over his head.

"What were you planning to do? Send me a post-card?"

"Actually," he said quietly, "I was hoping to persuade you to come with me."

She stared in the mirror, not sure she'd heard right, as he came up behind her, filling all the space in the glass and in her head too.

"I know. I know it's short notice! Believe me, I would have preferred to work up to the idea gradually. But events haven't left us much time, have they?'' His eyes searched hers, the pupils deep and intense. ''Will you, March? Come back with me to B.C.?''

"To live?'' Her thoughts spun. Did he know what he was asking? What exactly *was* he asking? ''For good, are you talking about? Leave Weatherfield and everything here?''

"Is that such an outrageous idea?''

Wrapping long arms about her, he pulled her close. "I'm in love with you, March. In case you hadn't realized. And unless I'm reading the signs wrong, you're in love with me.'' She nodded, conscious of his muscular warmth pressed against her back. ''Come and live with me, March,'' he said huskily, over the top of her head. ''Share the rest of my life with me.''

The breath caught in her throat. ''Marry you, you mean?''

"Women still do, I take it. Marry men?''

"Yes,'' she said weakly. Commitment—what she had wanted from Hunt and despaired of receiving. Now she was the one holding back.

"So I've heard,'' she said. ''Only—Hunt, how can I?'' she burst out. ''What about Marchmaids? My business! The cottage!''

His arms tightened, his lips nuzzled her neck, setting off another dizzying wave of sensations she was struggling to suppress.

"Mmm. Lemon and fresh ironing,'' he murmured. "You could sell the cottage. Start a new agency in B.C. People's houses need cleaning in all kinds of places besides Weatherfield.''

All kinds of places—that was the trouble! She

caught a glimpse of herself, following Hunt across the continents, leaving a trail of abandoned homes and agencies in her wake. Resentment, and something sharper she suspected might be plain unvarnished terror, pricked her.

"Be realistic, Hunt. You don't even have a place for us to live." That sounded lame and she tried to make a joke out of it. "Unless we set up housekeeping over your parents' garage."

"We could do worse. Right on the ocean," he teased in a voice like warm honey. "We've already got dishes. And a sleeping bag. Us together always—isn't that what you said was important?"

She nodded, her ability to speak temporarily mislaid.

He turned her around in his arms to face him and she saw that his quirked smile was full of tenderness. Her hand stole up of its own volition to smooth the crumpled collar of his shirt. A shirt that picked up the color of his eyes. She loved him, oh yes—enough to marry. Except for the voice in her head, clamoring to be heard.

"The part about waking up next to you would be heaven, I know, but—"

His fingers closed over hers. "And the other parts? Which ones aren't you sure about? Sharing the toothpaste? Deciding how to spend our Sundays?"

"Hunt, be serious!" Standing face-to-face with him didn't make thinking any easier, not when he was looking at her with his heart in his eyes. "Maybe not the toothpaste, or the Sundays, but stray dogs and guests who stay and accidents on the rugs—"

"We'll have hardwood floors."

"We're so different, you and I—"

"Good heavens, woman!" She could see he was trying hard not to lose patience. "Haven't I spent the last two weeks proving I can be as neat as the next guy? And as ruthless, when it comes to saying no?"

Neat, ruthless—She gave an involuntary shiver.

"Hunt, that's not the real you." If it were, she wouldn't love him as she did. The insight jolted her. "I don't want you trying to be something you're not. I know I couldn't be. It wouldn't last." She smiled to take the sting out of her assessment, but she couldn't do much about the misgivings in her eyes. "You're gregarious and hospitable. You attract people in need the way a sunny window attracts spots. And I'm a woman who makes a career of spotless homes. How long do you think, before we started sniping at each other again?"

"I'll take that risk," he said stubbornly. "Anything else?"

She looked at him. "Well, yes. Since you ask. This rolling stone thing you do. Always looking for new horizons. Hunt, I don't want to end up housekeeping on some rock somewhere in a . . . a tent."

He made a funny, fond face. "Have you seen the new ones? All modern conveniences. Plus great sunsets."

"Mosquitoes, too, I bet. Hungry bears and three-day rains."

He sighed and let go of her hand. "Are you turning me down?"

"No. Yes. Oh, Hunt—I don't want to, only—"

"I thought I was offering you marriage," he said softly. "I had no idea it was deprivation."

"Hunt, I can't live without a proper home! Stability.

Roots. All the things Margaret and I worked hard to keep. Now you're asking me to give them up?''

''I won't beg,'' he said after a moment.

''No.''

She wouldn't beg either. Not outwardly. It was all too sudden, too much . . . maybe if he could have given her more time. Helplessly, she waited by the door while he opened the night table drawer and removed a familiar envelope.

''The postdated checks,'' he said, holding them out to her. ''You might as well take them back. Since I won't be here anymore.''

''If all you're going to do is stare out the window, then I don't think refusing Hunt Reynolds was worth it.''

March flushed and swiveled her chair around.

A shower of sparrows in serviceable gray-brown uniforms had rained down on the lawn and she'd been watching them peck at the dry fall grass. Hunt no doubt would have fed the birds if he'd stayed till December. Bought great big sacks of sunflower seeds or whatever it was birds liked, and held open house for everything on wings in the neighborhood.

''I thought you didn't like Hunt,'' she told Anna Rose.

''I like you. And I can see the effect turning down his proposal is having on you.''

''It wasn't a real proposal.'' Just a heavenly half-baked idea that would never have worked.

Anna Rose looked up from the other side of the desk where she was juggling names and times. Not only The Cedars, but a lot of other customers were trickling back into the fold, and the schedule was in constant need of tinkering.

"Anyway, I never said I didn't like the man. I just didn't care for what he was doing to you."

"Well, he's stopped doing it. And I'm fine," snapped March.

"Then how come the week is half over, and you still haven't gone to do estimates for the people who responded to our free oven-cleaning?"

March groaned and flung a glance at the clock. Five past five; too late now. "I'll get on it tomorrow. First thing. Don't you ever go home anymore?" She had an unpleasant notion Anna Rose was hanging around just to keep an eye on her.

She was right about one thing, March reflected, watering her plants after a sketchy supper and discovering drought conditions in the pots. This wasn't working.

Ever since her final encounter with Hunt, she'd been existing in a kind of limbo. Household routines, prospective customers—Marchmaids itself, now that they were emerging from the financial woods—weren't important anymore. All she could think about was Hunt. Hunt leaving. Hunt asking her to come with him. To share his life. Her heart constricted at the thought. Late in the night, sitting up in bed, she dropped the book she'd been trying unsuccessfully to read and hugged her knees. Staring into the lamplight, she gave up the battle and let Hunt's presence wash over her, strong and laughing and tender. The sensation of Hunt's arms holding her close, and his kisses that she was giving up. For what?

She awoke before the alarm went off Thursday. Her face in the cheval glass looked pale but calm. As though she'd been through an illness and now the fever was gone. In the kitchen she made herself herbal tea and watched the first rays of sun touch her grandmother's cranberry glass while she waited for it to steep.

Quite possibly she could go on living without him. She'd find the strength somewhere, just as she and Margaret had found it to build a life for themselves after their parents died. But she'd be turning her back on what it meant to be a woman, whole and fulfilled. No business was worth that, and no house, either. Hunt was willing to risk their differences, why couldn't she? So what if he moved around a lot and took in strays? He made them seem like good things to be doing, in spite of the inconveniences—and they'd be doing them together. He made love seem like a good thing, the very best. The only thing.

Amazing, she thought, dialing Anna Rose's number on the kitchen phone, how the solution presented itself once you made up your mind. No, Tony hadn't left for work yet, said Anna Rose in reply to March's query, and yes, he could stop by the house with her.

"Any special reason? March, you sound different."

"Tell you when you get here," she said, and hung up. Humming, she ran up the stairs to shower and hunt in the closet for the new white blouse she'd been holding in reserve.

"Thanks for making time," she said, ushering the Tremontis into the kitchen half an hour later. Tony, in clean denim and with his springy black curls temporarily tamed, grinned.

"Beats starting the day at the garage," he said.

"I'll keep it short," March promised, as Anna Rose slid onto the bench and patted the seat for him to join her. Her gray eyes were suspicious. "This has something to do with Hunt Reynolds, doesn't it?" she demanded. "You even *look* different this morning."

March laughed. "Let's just say it's because I've decided to make changes in my life." Best to come straight to the point, she thought, nervous in spite of herself at the expectant look on their faces. "Anna Rose, how would you feel about running Marchmaids on your own?"

"On my own?" She sat up. "Why would you want me to? What would you be doing?"

"I'm getting to that—"

"This *is* about Hunt, isn't it?" Anna Rose looked at her as though she were some kind of traitor. "Don't tell me you've changed your mind about going off with him! March, I know I said some hasty things. But do you honestly think it's a good idea—"

"To ask you to take over Marchmaids?" March smiled. "I think it's a fantastic idea! The business would go on the same as now and everybody would get to keep their job. Except that you'd be in charge. With your experience and common sense, there's no reason you can't manage as well as I do."

"I didn't mean—" Anna Rose took a deep breath. "You really think so? It's an awful responsibility."

"You're running a major part of the service as it is. It would would mean more money, of course. And I'd only be as far as the telephone. B.C. isn't the other side of the moon."

"That's not what you were saying a few days ago," Anna Rose reminded her. She exchanged glances with Tony. "I don't know. We'd have to discuss it first—"

"Naturally. That's why I wanted Tony to be in on

this. I'm aware it would involve more of your time and you'd need his support.''

''She'd have that,'' declared Tony. Pride shone in his eyes. ''I agree with March, Rosie. You could handle the job. And I'd be pleased to see you get the chance.'' He patted her hand. ''Still, it's your decision to make.''

She nodded, pink-cheeked, and March felt a twinge of—what? Envy? This was how a partnership between two people who loved each other should be; each willing to give, each respecting the abilities of the other. If she could achieve that with Hunt . . . Her face must have betrayed her wistfulness, because Anna Rose was saying, ''March, are you positive? Think about the kind of life you'd be getting into. You could end up a nomad, for heaven's sake!''

''In that case, I'd set up Marchmaids franchises coast to coast. Who knows, worldwide!''

Tony laughed and hitched himself to his feet. ''Every one of them a success, too—I'd bet on it. It's March's life, Rosie. We've got a decision of our own to make, remember?''

The staff was arriving as he climbed into the pickup truck and they exchanged cheerful calls and laughter. The women all knew Tony. Some of them wouldn't have minded trading places with Anna Rose and said so openly. Bettina, first in the change room, poked noisily through her locker.

''What was *he* doing here? You guys holding a hush-hush management meeting or something?''

March pretended not to hear. They'd been worried enough about their jobs lately. Time to tell them about changes when they were certain. The teams seemed to take forever to leave.

"Does Hunt know yet?" asked Anna Rose the minute they were alone.

"Not yet. I'm going over to The Cedars now."

Anna Rose kept her eyes on the telephone memo in her hand. A new customer from Warbler Woods—the big second chance they'd been waiting for. "You honestly think it could work out between you and Hunt?"

"I'll never know if I don't try."

"And if you don't try, you'll regret it the rest of your life."

March gave her arm a squeeze, her fingers cold with apprehension. Anna Rose might have her doubts, but she understood. She was in love herself and she'd follow Tony to Patagonia without a murmur, if that was where he wanted to go. "You'll tell me, when you've made a decision concerning the job?"

"This afternoon. I'm meeting Tony for lunch." She gave March a sad-hopeful look. "What can I say? I'd lend you my earrings, only they didn't do you much good the first time."

Buttoning her blazer in front of the hall mirror after Anna Rose had left, she ran a critical eye over her appearance. Maybe the new March should have worn something more adventurous. She pushed her hair behind her ear and her blue eyes stared back, unnaturally bright. On the brink of joy or the brink of tears.

In the car she fretted over whether she should have phoned first. She grimaced at an elderly station wagon ambling along ahead of her and fumed at the lights. Now that she was on her way every second's delay seemed a second wasted. Hunt. She said his name out loud like a talisman, and rehearsed the words she would use to tell him.

The Range Rover wasn't in The Cedars' drive.

But Margaret's sporty little Mazda was, glinting in the morning sun. So they were back! March parked and ran up the step between the geranium trees. Maybe Hunt had gone with Rene to the gallery, or maybe he was at the university, clearing out his desk.

Margaret beamed as she swung open the door. "March! I was just about to give you a call. We got in last night."

"Lovely to have you back, Maggie!" The vestibule smelled of Dior scent as they hugged. "Although under the circumstances, I'm sure you'd prefer not to be."

Margaret gave a dramatic sigh and rolled amethyst eyes. She had a fluffy new hairdo and looked marvelous. Europe had evidently agreed with her. "I still can't quite believe what happened. Rene's out conferring with the police or insurance agents or whoever. Fortunately we brought back the most marvelous replacements. Wait till I tell you! Join me for breakfast and we'll talk," she said, leading the way to the solarium.

March trailed in her wake. Margaret was in her dressing gown, a gossamer creation appliquéd with silver butterflies. "I'm early, I'm afraid," she said, her eyes searching the atrium for evidence of Hunt.

"Nonsense! I've been up ages. Getting a start on the unpacking. Hunt left at the crack of dawn and Rene soon after. For heaven's sake, March! Don't stand there—you're at home." She smiled and waved a hand at the table invitingly set under the bougainvillea. "Toast? A muffin? We discovered the most delicious honey in Holland—"

March shook her head. The room was sharp with the colors of the flowers in the sun. For a moment she thought she might be sick, the smell of coffee and orange blossoms was so strong.

"Hunt left this morning?" she managed to say, pulling out a chair. "For B.C., you mean?"

"I assume so. I never thought to ask. He had the Range Rover all packed and ready last night. You'll have coffee, at least?" she urged, holding up a blue-patterned cup. The Royal Copenhagen was back in use, and why not? It was safe now.

"Rene tried to persuade him to stay a couple of days, but he was on hot coals to be gone. Well, I don't have to tell you! You know by now what Hunt Reynolds is like with his mind made up." Margaret's eyes, exquisitely outlined because she never faced the day without makeup, studied her across the table. She knew her too well not to realize something was wrong. "The team is still coming Saturday? Hunt didn't do anything outrageous to—"

"No, no. They're coming."

Margaret nodded.

"Funny, when I think how I didn't trust Rene's choice of a house sitter, and that's the one thing that turned out well."

March mumbled a few noncommittal words. Someday she'd tell her sister the whole roller-coaster story of events at The Cedars and they'd both have a good laugh. But not now.

"Of course you were smart to pack away the breakable stuff—why didn't I think of that? Which reminds me, I bought you something in Bruges! Have a muffin, while I see if I can lay my hands on it."

As if she could swallow food! She had trouble even summoning up pleasure when Margaret dropped the tissue-wrapped package in her lap. Inside was a nightgown of flowing eggshell satin with a lace bodice Cleopatra might have coveted.

"Are you sure? It's lovely. But not quite what—"

"You'd want to wear to bed alone. Exactly! Call it a hint."

She flushed and thought of Hunt. His image was so strong inside her that she couldn't keep from saying his name.

"Did Hunt leave a phone number?" she said, making a big production of folding the gown and dismayed to find her hands trembling. "Someplace where he could be reached?"

"No. I don't suppose he knew himself, yet." Margaret looked at her shrewdly. The butter knife hung poised in her pearl-tipped fingers. "He promised to call you before he left, didn't he?" she asked.

"Not really." March scraped back her chair. The lump in her throat was threatening to dissolve into tears. Margaret was always good at putting two and two together. Her sympathy would only make things worse.

"I could ask Rene to track him down, if you like. Or get in touch with his parents. Pass on a message for you . . ."

"Heavens no!" It wasn't the type of message you could pass on by way of a third person, even if you wanted to. The fountain in the atrium glittered and she realized the tears had risen as far as her eyes. Beside her, Margaret chattered tactfully about fountains in Europe. Poetry in stone, set in the heart of those centuries-old town squares, she said. "Someday, March, you must travel, the world is so full of beautiful things."

No, not without Hunt, she thought.

"Actually," Margaret went on, "Rene was a bit disappointed in Hunt. Leaving when we'd hardly said hello! Rene joked about it. He wondered if—" She hesitated. *They wondered if he was in a hurry to get away from some woman,* thought March, *only she doesn't like to say in case it might be me.*

"It's all right, Maggie. Really it is." She got out her car keys. "I'll come by in a day or two. To hear the details of your trip."

Her sister saw her off from the step, rubbing her hands over her silken arms in the brisk fall air. "Remember, if you want to talk, I'm here for you. Nothing's changed."

"I know." But it *had* changed. She smiled shakily over the top of the car door. "I'm a big girl now and I've got to deal with this on my own." Margaret gave a rueful nod and March turned the key in the ignition.

Hunt had warned her he wouldn't beg, and she hadn't expected him to. But he could have called to say good-bye and check if she'd changed her mind. She wouldn't have been the first woman to do so! She swung into Parkway Drive and accelerated. Unless of course he'd thought it over and decided he'd had a lucky escape and it was better this way. A good thing the old March had picked up the list of prospective customers as she left the office. Stopping at the nearest pay phone, she fished it out of her bag and thrust a coin in the slot. Three of the five people were at home. Hunt wasn't the only one lucky today.

She got through the morning working out estimates with a tight professional smile clamped over her feelings. Purposely, she timed her return to Emery Street for noon to avoid running into Anna Rose. Pitying questions were the last thing she needed right now.

The rush of anger had begun to subside. A feeling of loss bored deep as she let herself into the silent house.

She'd waited too long to make up her mind; no use blaming Hunt for *that*. The story of their relationship, that she always seemed to be two steps behind him! She heated a bowl of soup she didn't really want, and carried it into the office. There was still a chance at the last minute he'd left a message on the answering machine.

But he hadn't. Nothing.

The afternoon stretched before her like a desert. So did the rest of her life. She switched off the machine and entertained wild thoughts about flying out to B.C. Looking up his parents and camping on the steps of his room over the garage till he showed up. She'd be homeless and he'd have to take her in, wouldn't he? He'd laugh at the irony but she could take that. She pushed aside her half-empty bowl and on the telephone pad underneath, Anna Rose had written in capital letters:

MARCH! NEW CUSTOMER—COUNTING ON US! 4 STORIES. I GAVE MY WORD YOU'D DO AN ESTIMATE THIS AFT. HIGHWAY 4 WEST OF WEATHERFIELD.

She frowned. Anna Rose *knew* they never took out-of-town jobs—travel time ate up the profits. She'd neglected to give a name and phone number after the directions. Instead, she'd drawn a happy face and the words *Champagne for lunch?!* A state of mind that explained the mistake and triggered in March a strong desire to burst into tears.

Chapter Eleven

She had forgotten about her offer this morning—
Anna Rose would be shattered when she withdrew it.
Well, this had turned into a day for disappointments
and why should anyone be spared? March reached
tiredly for her bag. Since she couldn't phone, she'd
have to drive out in person and tell the four-story customer thanks, but no thanks. Who had four stories out
in the country, anyway? It sounded crazy.

The red-roofed variety store and gas bar at the in-
terchange looked familiar. With a shock March recognized the highway Hunt had taken to Summer Bay
at Thanksgiving.

The trees had been scarlet and gold that day, mirroring the festive way she'd felt, sitting next to him
with the music rollicking and his eyes relaying heady
secrets. Now the branches were shorn and Hunt was
speeding westward alone. The worst part was not
knowing, was it pride, or pain, or lack of sufficient
love on his part that spurred him on his way? Farms
huddled ready for winter. A long spear of water glim-
mered across the fields—Lake Huron. Somewhere
here she was supposed to turn off. Slowing at a junc-
tion she glimpsed, behind a row of poplars, the lighthouse.

Her heart began to pound as she made the turn.
Anna Rose had gotten the directions wrong as well as

everything else and through some uncanny coincidence they'd landed her here. Nobody lived at the lighthouse—only ghosts in the long grass, and the sooner she got away the the better. As she reached for the clutch, a wisp of smoke drifted up up from the chimney of the white frame house.

Her hand froze. A yellow dog bounded out from under the trees, barking and waving a plumed tail. March switched off the engine and tumbled out of the car, seized by a wild hope.

"Noble? Is that you?"

She felt foolish asking. But the dog was delighted she remembered his name and let her bury her hands in his silky ruff. With Noble at her heels, she started toward the house. Parked around the side, was the Range Rover.

A man appeared on the verandah. He had big sloping shoulders and sunlit hair and was unmistakably Hunt. She stumbled and caught herself, as joy threatened to engulf her.

"Marchmaids. Reliable as ever," he said gruffly, and leaped down the steps to meet her.

"Hunt." For a moment she had the feeling he was going to wrap his arms around her and swing her off her feet and she was going to let him. But then both of them hung back.

"What are you doing here?" she said. It came out sounding like an accusation. "I thought you were on your way back to B.C."

"Would you care if I were?"

That sounded like an accusation, too, and she felt the need to defend herself. "I don't know why I should. After the misery you put me through!"

He studied her gravely. His face looked as though

he'd been through a few sleepless nights himself. "I imagine it's similar to what you put me through. I was beginning to wonder, whether my lighthouse idea would be enough to salvage the situation."

"Your . . . lighthouse idea?" She darted a look around, distracted by the pleasing implications of the fact that he'd suffered as she had. A bag of dog kibble leaned against the railing next to a mop and pail. Music wafted through the open door. Ludwig's Pastoral, she guessed, catching a flute note of birdsong.

She followed him up the steps like a woman hypnotized. "What are you talking about, lighthouse idea? Hunt, what are you *doing* here?"

He laughed and waved her inside. "Hasn't the other shoe dropped yet? I live here. Welcome to my new home, March."

"Your home!" The pegged maple floor shifted underfoot.

They were in the room she'd glimpsed that day through the window. A crackling warmth radiated from the stove and a pot of something that smelled of herbs and onions burbled on top. Beethoven was performing from a smart new china hutch and a matching table and chairs held pride of place in front of a window overlooking the lake. Most astonishing of all, the table was set for two, with the ironstone seagulls looking in their element at last.

"You mean—you've bought this place?" March stared at him, her thoughts spinning. "To live in? A lighthouse?"

"Signed the papers two days ago. My first mortgage. Shopped for the basics, moved in, and here I am."

"I'm speechless. I—I don't know what to say."

She reached for a chair and sank down. Her knees felt spongy. She wasn't sure whether his news or being near him, affected her more. "Hunter J. Reynolds with a mortgage. Property, furniture! It seems, well, out of character."

He leaned against a counter. "So you keep telling me." He sent her a long look, the kind that made her cheeks feel hot. "How do you know the other Hunt— the homeless wanderer—wasn't the one out of character?"

"But what about B.C.? Breakers on the shore? New horizons? How will you live, for heaven's sake? You've given up your class at Weatherfield U!"

"They offered me a post as department head. Part of the reshuffling I mentioned? I told them I'd reconsidered and would be pleased to accept. As for horizons—" He gestured to where the lake rippled vast and shining to the rim of the sky. "Enough there to last a lifetime. Breakers, too, on a stormy day. Plus, I get to keep my dog."

Noble thumped an agreeable tail on the new braided mat by the stove. Shakily, March took off her blazer and hung it over the back of the chair. "I'm sure he missed you as much you missed him," she said. *As much as I missed you,* she added silently. He hadn't mentioned her part yet in this fresh scheme of things and she couldn't quite bring herself to ask.

Instead she said, "Why the lighthouse, Hunt? There must be other houses for sale overlooking the lake."

"Ah." His eyes danced with some pleasure he hadn't yet shared with her. "But only a lighthouse can deliver what I'm looking for. A built-in system ready made to accomodate opposing lifestyles. Come on— I'll show you what I mean."

His hand closed around hers, warm and strong as he pulled her to her feet, and the anxious knot inside her began to loosen.

"Starting with the kitchen. Perfect for communal activities like cooking and eating. Socializing. Of course it still needs a microwave and a dishwasher— the old Hunt hasn't quite bowed out of the picture." He flashed her a conspiratorial grin. "And through here—" He threw open a door and gestured. "—the original bedrooms, with bath across the hall. Made to order for putting up those hard-luck overnight guests."

She shot him a look. "Homeless students, you mean? Old flames?"

"Students, yes. Old flames, no. Too combustible. Every home needs fire regulations, and this one's iron-clad."

"Tell me more," she said, warming to his game.

"Next the lighthouse tower." He flourished an oversized brass key and unlocked a recessed door. "Fully private, you'll notice, and by invitation only. Ms. Briarwood?" he said with a bow, and waited for her to step inside the round sunny room.

"Unfurnished yet, so you'll have to use your imagination." A carton of his books spilled over onto the flagstone floor. "The study, I thought. Bookshelves all around. Rugs. A couple of easy chairs and a desk at either window. His and hers," he threw over his shoulder, and headed for the staircase hugging the wall.

She nodded, glad he hadn't waited for her comment. She didn't think she'd have been capable of making one at the moment.

"The trouble at The Cedars was, all the living space is on one level," he said, long legs pumping. "Which made it too darn easy for people and animals to spread. Whereas in a lighthouse, you've got these steep, winding stairs to form natural barriers. Living room, would you say?''

The view from the windows was straight out of a travel brochure. Village roofs tumbled out of the trees and down the hill to the marina, where boats like toys rode at anchor. Across the lake, the sun was making spectacular preparations to sink into the state of Michigan.

''Definitely. The living room.'' She turned. His and hers, he'd said. Dreamily she pictured the two of them. ''With cushioned window seats. Sectional sofa to take advantage of the view. Coffee table sturdy enough to support a man's feet.'' She glanced at him from under her lashes. ''I don't imagine you were planning to shop for those on your own,'' she said.

''I was hoping to get help. From somebody who knows her way around Weatherfield Mall.''

She smiled. Life spread out before her. Like the lake, shimmering with possibilities. ''And the top levels? What did you have in mind for them?''

''Come and find out, why don't you?''

They went up the stairs hand in hand. ''An en suite bath next, I thought. Whirlpool tub over there . . .'' She completed the image for him. ''Overhung by scarlet bougainvillea.''

He laughed, the warm sound she loved. ''How did you guess? Dressing room adjacent with plenty of closets.''

''His and hers,'' she repeated, for the sheer pleasure of it.

''And now, best for last.'' His eyes struck sparks from hers as they climbed. ''The master bedroom.''

The flood of light at the top of the stairs nearly lifted her off her feet. Hunt's face was golden with it, and his familiar forearms she had to stop herself from touching. She felt out of breath in a way that had nothing to do with the climb or even the view.

"Can't you see it? Your crimson poppies on the bed—"

"Or the duvet."

"Mmm." His arm stole around her waist. "You'll have me giving up the sleeping bag next. On hot summer nights," he murmured in her ear, "there's always the observation deck, for sleeping under the stars." He indicated the ceiling, where a folding ladder flanked a trapdoor. "Naturally in winter, when the wind howls—" His hand moved lower on her hip and pulled her snugly close. "—it'll be cozier bedding down in front of the woodstove."

She nodded, almost bowled over by a rush of physical longing to be lying there with him right now.

"When did you decide all this, Hunt? Not to go back to B.C. To stay and find a house—a lighthouse," she corrected herself, "and settle down instead?"

"On the weekend. After you left and I felt about as devastated as a man can feel. That's when it struck me—why move on when everything I want is here?" He turned her around to face him, hands gentle, and their eyes locked. His pupils darkened with emotion. "How come, I thought, March is the one who has to make all the compromises? When I'm the one who wants to make her happy." He wasn't smiling. He looked as earnest as she'd ever seen him. "What do you think, March? Could you be happy here with me?"

"Doing a little lighthouse-keeping, you mean?"

Tenderness vied with amusement in his face. "Have I told you that I love you?" He paused and the earnestness returned. "Let's get one thing straight. I don't want you for the cleaning. We'll hire a team to do that. From this A-1 agency I know."

"Marchmaids?" she said.

"That's the one. You realize, with Weatherfield only half an hour away, you'll be able to keep the agency. And the cottage to run it from."

She looked at him, at the features she'd conjured up a thousand times and never loved so profoundly as she did at this moment. "Do you know where I was this morning when you left your message? At The Cedars. To tell you Anna Rose was taking over, and I was ready to come to B.C. with you."

He made a sound in his throat.

"Forgive me, March. I should have let you know earlier. But when the days went by and I didn't hear from you—Call it male pride! I decided I had to have everything in place before I laid it at your feet. To lessen the chances of you turning me down."

"Is that why you didn't let Anna Rose give the name of the four-story customer?" She smiled and then instantly sobered. "You could still change your mind. About staying. Now that I've told you—"

"No!" His reply was gratifyingly quick. "You've only confirmed that my decision was the right one."

His eyes burned into her soul as he lowered his head and kissed her. Or perhaps she reached up and kissed him. All her life, she thought, had been leading up to this moment. His hands pulling her close, her arms lifting to twine themselves about his neck. Warm tide sweeping her along, swelling into an aching fiery need to slip deeper into his embrace. He was the one who drew back, his breathing ragged.

"We can watch the sunset together. And the sunrise."

The light in the room had turned from gold to rose. So had the sky outside. But his face was the only thing she wanted to see.

"Are you still thinking of asking me to marry you?" she said innocently.

His whole body stilled. "I . . . March, will you?"

"Is that a lifetime contract we're talking?"

"What do you think?" he said.

She smiled and her body relaxed against his, filled suddenly with that Saturday feeling. The whole world neat and polished and shipshape, and nothing to do except be happy.

Charlotte County Library
P.O. Box 788
Charlotte C.H., VA 23923